TEXAS COWBOY'S BRIDE

BARB HAN

TORJAKE PUBLISHING

Editing: Ali Williams

Cover Design: Jacob's Cover Designs

For my family. I'm so fortunate to get to do life with each of you. My love for you has no bounds and I count my blessings every day.
And to Barbara Griffin and all the rockstar single mothers out there. In case no one has mentioned it, you are doing an amazing job.

1

C hloe Brighton flipped on her headlights. Darkness descended on the small Texas town where she'd grown up as she navigated the familiar backroads toward the high-way, Austin, and home. Time had gotten away from her. It was well after eight o'clock. She'd hoped to get home before dusk.

Leaving what had been her family home without answers about her brother felt wrong on so many levels. She didn't—couldn't—believe he'd taken his own life three days ago. There was no way that the person she knew would have written a suicide note and disap-peared, even though she couldn't deny the handwriting belonged to him. No one could convince her that he would intentionally write those words because Nicholas Brighton would never have apologized in that way, nor would he take his own life.

When her brother had stopped returning her calls and texts, she'd phoned the sheriff for a wellness check on her brother. She'd expected to learn that her brother had relapsed and didn't want her to know he was drinking; instead, she'd learned of a suicide note followed by an intense search for her brother's body on her family's property. The house had been cordoned off with crime scene tape and turned over. The sheriff had issued a Be On The Lookout, but her brother wasn't found, and his body wasn't recovered, leaving her in limbo. More of those tears threatened.

Chloe shelved those thoughts before the onslaught of tears came. She needed to focus on the road, on getting back to her apartment so she could process the fact his dog had been found and yet he was still missing. She glanced at the backseat where Zeus lay in a ball, exhausted. Even he'd seemed reluctant to leave Gunner. Three days of searching for her brother had netted zero.

At the intersection, she sat with her blinker on. A right turn would shave twenty minutes off her drive. Left would take her past the Quinn family ranch. Aiden Quinn had been her best friend in high school. And even though he'd left years ago without looking back, the thought of seeing his family ranch again was comforting. Impulse took over and she turned left.

Since she was running late anyway, what would a few more minutes hurt? She'd decided to take the long road out of a bout of nostalgia and not a bone-deep ache to see her old best friend again. At least that was the lie she tried to tell herself.

There'd been something special about the period of time in her life when they'd been close that had been different, simple. Not long after graduation, she'd moved to Austin for college and Aiden moved away for good. Her brother had one year of school left before he planned to join her. Then, her parents had died in a crash. Her brother finished his senior year of high school by staying with a friend's family before changing plans and signing up for the military.

Based on what she'd heard of Aiden, he never looked back at Gunner. Thinking about him caused a familiar stab of pain that she'd tucked away long ago. He and his self-made millionaire cattle rancher father had never seen eye-to-eye. Something, and she wasn't sure what, had happened to push Aiden over the edge. The likelihood of running into him now was almost laughable, although the thought of being near his family home calmed her.

In the passenger seat next to her, she touched the folded flag and then ran her fingers along the letters of her brother's dog tags that were sitting on top. Nicholas's dog, Zeus, was still curled in a ball in the back seat, sleeping. A neighbor had spotted him not long after her brother's disappearance, but it had taken days of persistence to corral him into her yard.

Zeus whimpered in the backseat. She risked another glance at him. He was asleep but unsettled. Was he dreaming? Her brother had had him for a little more than a month, but the two had become best friends, according to Nicholas. If she remembered correctly, he'd used the words *soul mates*. She wanted to offer some reassurance, some sense of comfort to Zeus, but came up empty.

"You're okay, buddy." It wasn't much, but it was the best she could offer. She'd retrieved one of her brother's shirts from his laundry hamper for Zeus to lay his head on and another to wear, hoping the German shepherd might find some comfort in his owner's scent. Her brother had loved his dog. Zeus was another reason Chloe was convinced that her brother couldn't have taken his own life because it would've meant leaving his dog. That's not something her brother would have done.

Nicholas may have stopped trusting people and she could admit he'd lost faith in humanity to a very large degree after coming home from his tour, but he'd perked up the minute he picked up Zeus and brought him home. Zeus had quickly become Nicholas's best friend. And now, Zeus was all she had left of the brother she couldn't seem to reach even though she never stopped trying.

Emotion welled in her chest and she blinked back fresh tears that threatened to spill down her cheeks. The past six months had been hard after her brother had come home to Gunner. The hope, the light, that came with his recent improvements had been obliterated with the news he was gone.

Feeling the weight of the dog tags against her skin, headlights caught her attention on the two-lane highway they'd dubbed *Quinn-land Road*. Up ahead, the pair of white orbs grew as they came barreling down the highway. "Come on, guy. Tone down your lights."

Chloe brought her left arm up to shield her eyes. The dog tags were firmly gripped in her right hand along with the steering wheel. She was used to crazy drivers. Austin traffic was basically a never-ending rush hour. The city had two speeds: breakneck and crawl. This guy would fit right in with the first group.

All she could do was slow down and yield. She eased to the right as far as she could without her tires hitting gravel on the shoulder. Still, the guy's lights practically blinded her. Did he have on his high beams? She flashed hers at him, trying to alert him to the fact he was making it impossible for her to see. A split-second too late, she realized the vehicle had veered left into her lane and was going to hit her.

The next few minutes played out in slow motion. The airbag deployed. She screamed for Zeus. She could've sworn she'd heard him yelp, and then a thud sounded and the driver's seat took a jolt. Before she could turn around to get a look at him, her door opened, and she was being jerked out by a substantial man.

The strong as an ox guy wore all black. Sunglasses covered his eyes, a hoodie concealed his hair, and she couldn't make out any of his other features clearly. He was angry...*no*...determined.

Instinctively, she put her hands down to stop her fall, skinning her wrists in the process. The burn was nothing compared to the pain rocketing through her when her head hit the pavement.

A low growl ripped from Zeus's throat, and then she heard him cry out. Determination welled inside her as she tried to push up to all fours and get to her brother's dog. A strong, masculine hand dug into her hair at the crown of her head.

"Where do you think you're going?" The unfamiliar man's voice came out as practically a growl.

"Leave my dog alone. Don't you dare hurt him." There was no way she could lose Zeus.

When the only response that came was a blow to the back of her head, dread settled over her, weighing down her limbs. She saw stars. This guy was strong. Nausea gripped her as her vision blurred. Chloe was in trouble.

"What do you want from me? My wallet? Take it. Take my purse. Just leave my dog alone." Reaching up to touch her head where it felt like it had been split in two, her hand was slapped away before she could reach her hairline.

Even with a spike of adrenaline she struggled to stay conscious and alert. The thought occurred to her that she would need to be able to provide details to law enforcement. Glancing up, she saw the man had on a black tracksuit.

With a vise-like grip, he forced her to face the ground. Her gaze darted around, searching for any sign of Zeus. Where could he be and why was he suddenly being so quiet?

Please, God, let him have run away. She repeated a silent protection prayer that she'd learned as a young girl in Sunday school. All she could do now was count feet. There was one pair of shoes. She listened for sounds of another person and heard something to her right. From her peripheral, she tried to follow the sound but came up short.

Another blow to the back of her head with a blunt instrument and she dropped flat onto the concrete. A little voice inside her told her to play dead.

In a surprising move, she felt a big hand poke at the spot where it felt like her head had cracked in two. She grunted when no words came.

"She's bleeding." The unfamiliar voice was a little bit clearer this time. She noted a Cajun accent. Louisiana? She searched her memory bank, wishing, praying she could figure out who this was and why he'd want to hurt her.

Trying to move her mouth to speak was useless. It was a strange sensation to say the least, being able to hear her thoughts so clearly and yet not be able to voice them.

"You idiot. Why'd you hit the back of her head? Now, it'll be harder to cover up. This just got messy." There was no luck with the second voice, either. Both sounded muffled, like they were standing in a tunnel.

As the men argued, she forced her eyes to open and scan the area for Zeus. Where could he be? She called out to him in her mind but realized her mouth still wasn't working and even if it was, shouting would be a bad idea. An overwhelming feeling that she was about to be sick to her stomach caused her to gasp.

With the men preoccupied, she wondered if she could figure out an escape. She squinted, barely able to make out their large frames as they went to work, pulling something toward her vehicle. Zeus? She stifled a sob. Whatever it was, it was large. Too large to be Zeus?

God, she prayed so.

And then it came. An opportunity to make a move. Both of the men's backs were turned to her. This was it. It was pretty much now or never. The only question was whether or not she had enough strength to pull off a maneuver.

Chloe took in a deep breath and repeated the mantra *now or never.* She rolled underneath her SUV and through to the other side expecting to hear one of the men shout at her or each other. When neither did, she scanned the area for Zeus and figured he must've run off scared. He wasn't himself. He missed Nicholas. Finding her brother's dog was her number one priority as soon as she got out of sight. Thinking how scared he must be right now was a gut punch.

"Hey!" One of the jerks must've noticed that she'd disappeared.

As she rolled toward the nearby trees and scrub brush, she heard the familiar one calling the other a few choice names. She was so close to freedom that she could almost taste it. And yet, now that the jerks had realized she was on the move she feared she wouldn't make it in time.

And that's when she heard it. The low growl that she first thought might be coming from a wolf. Footsteps came toward her from behind as she pushed up on all fours and scurried toward the woods. All she could think about was getting away from those men and to safety. Branches slapped her face as she felt her way through the pitch-black woods, moving deeper and listening for sounds of Zeus. He wouldn't have growled at her, but he would have defended her against the jerks trying to hurt her if he'd been able. If he was out there, he could be injured. She couldn't risk calling out to him.

"Stop wherever you are. We'll find you and it'll be even worse. Don't make this hard on all of us." The voices came from the opposite direction of her. Her second break. How long before the men figured her out and changed course?

Chloe slowed her pace and moved as quietly as she could, afraid of whatever it was that had growled at her back there.

As the voices faded, her energy drained. If she sat down for a few minutes, she might get a lot farther. Sitting down ended up being more like a plunk. A tree branch jabbed her in the spine and she bit back the urge to scream.

Closing her eyes, she leaned her head against a tree. She could listen better this way. Her eyes kept drifting closed and it was getting harder to open them each time. Just another minute and she'd have enough strength to get up. With great effort, she curled onto her side and then clawed for purchase until she climbed into scrub brush for cover.

A moment later, everything went black.

2

Aiden Quinn exited the freeway, navigating onto the familiar two-lane highway toward his family's cattle ranch. He couldn't help but feel the area was stuck in a time warp. Even after ten years, the road leading to his hometown looked exactly the same.

Granted, it was nighttime, and visibility was limited to what he could see from the headlights lighting the path in front of him. Even so, there were no new houses, no construction to speak of.

As he drove through downtown, he took note of the same buildings. The square consisted of a post office, City Hall, and the feed store. There was a bakery next door to the inn, and a great lunch place. These were the kinds of establishments that had been passed down to family members for multiple generations. Most everyone was on a first-name basis in his hometown and knew his father. *Or at least they thought they did.*

Aiden had been summoned home on the basis that his father was about to make a life-changing announcement. Six out of seven brothers had made the trek home. It seemed Aiden was the holdout.

Considering the fact that he'd taken off after high school graduation without looking back, he had no idea what his father's life was like now, so he was clueless as to what the announcement might be. Several of Aiden's brothers were speculating their father's health might be declining. Not to be crass, but Aiden would believe it when he saw it. T.J. Quinn was made tough.

During Aiden's childhood, he couldn't remember his father taking a sick day. This announcement was most likely a trick so that T.J. could manipulate his sons. The others had come home and, much to his utter shock, were sticking around. Given the fact that his old man still ran the family cattle ranch, he figured not much had changed. A strained relationship with his father was one of many reasons Aiden preferred to keep Gunner in his rearview.

Shifting in the driver's seat, Aiden figured he had another twenty-minutes left of what had been a fifteen-hour drive from his home in Colorado, where he owned and operated a construction business that specialized in designing and building barns. If he'd timed his arrival correctly, he would miss bumping into his father tonight. Aiden figured it was best to get his bearings before facing that beast.

Life on the ranch started at four a.m., so folks would be retiring to their rooms for the evening. It wasn't that he didn't want to see his brothers—they were the only reason he'd made the drive from Colorado in the first place. But being back on the family property, and anywhere near the same vicinity as T.J. Quinn, was enough to digest for one day.

Aiden rubbed dry, blurry eyes. Up ahead in the distance, a stranded or abandoned vehicle caught his attention. Very few folks drove on this back road. The ones who did were usually lost, not stopped in the middle of the road with headlights on. He slowed down. As he got closer, he realized the vehicle was jackknifed across the two-lane highway.

The SUV's lights were still on even though he couldn't make out a driver. A car crash? One vehicle? He scanned the area for signs of the vehicle's occupants.

As he neared the site, he flipped on his high beams. There was a large lump in front of the SUV. He opened his door and stepped out, leaving the lights on. He expected to find someone in the SUV but didn't.

His cousin Griff, the sheriff, needed to know about this. Aiden fished his cell from his front pocket as he circled around the front of the SUV. There was a deer all right. He examined the point of impact on the vehicle, and made the call.

"Aiden, how long has it been?" The warmth and enthusiasm in Griff's voice was the best welcome.

"Too long." In the time since Aiden had left Gunner, Griff had taken over the job of sheriff from his father. That apple hadn't fallen far from the tree; a saying that didn't apply to Aiden and T.J.

"Are you home?" Griff asked.

"Close. I'm on the highway in between Quinnland and town. There's been a wreck. Someone hit a deer and," he checked in both directions, "I don't see a driver or passengers. The SUV looks to be abandoned. The way the deer is lying strikes me as strange." He'd heard of the recent crime wave in Gunner.

"I don't have to remind you to be careful with fingerprints. Do you see anything inside the vehicle that could help us identify the driver?" Shuffling noises came through the line and he could tell that his cousin was on the move.

"The driver's side door is open and the dome light is on." He walked around to look inside. The implication this could be something besides a car crash sat thickly in the air. Gunner had seen its fair share of crime recently. His brothers had kept him up to date because many had involved his family. "There's a purse inside that looks untouched."

"Okay. I'll be there in half an hour, maybe faster this time of night. Any chance you can stick around until then?"

He wasn't going anywhere. Because a lab coat embroidered with the name, Chloe, was wrapped around the driver's seat.

"Does Chloe Brighton still live in Gunner?"

"No. She lives in Austin now. Her brother does...*did* until recently."

The Brighton family had lived on the outskirts of Gunner and didn't come into town much as far as he remembered. He and Chloe had been thick as thieves, though. She'd talked him into letting her little brother tag along on fishing trips. He smiled at the memory. "Nicholas? How's he doing?"

"You haven't heard?" Griff's voice was low and respectful which sounded all kinds of warning sirens for Aiden.

"Nicholas left a suicide note and then disappeared."

Those words were a throat punch. Nicholas Brighton, Chloe's little brother? It was strange that Aiden thought the guy should still be seventeen-years-old and very much alive, like time had somehow stood still in his home town.

"Do you know his circumstances? What might drive him to make that decision?"

"Chloe was adamant that he wouldn't have. He ended the note with an apology. She claims her brother would never do that."

"From what I know of him that sounds right." Coach had tried to get him to write an apology to his teammates for some small infraction that Aiden couldn't remember anymore. It was standard practice. Nicholas had refused even after Coach threatened to bench him for the rest of the season. Nicholas had loved football to the point of obsession. He'd opted to sit out and Coach ended up giving him a different punishment.

"Did you know he'd joined the military after graduation?"

"I remember something about it." One of Aiden's older brothers had done the same. Isaac had signed up after graduation to get away from their father. There were too many stories of servicemen not being able to adjust to civilian life or, worse yet, cope with traumatic experiences. Aiden barely knew what was going on in his own family half the time but he remembered how protective Chloe had been of her younger brother. The fact that he was gone would've hit her hard. "Did something happen?"

"Nicholas ended his tour with a medical board. Lost his left leg from the knee down and part of his right hand." His service and sacrifice went beyond words.

Aiden was silent for a beat. His mind snapped to Chloe again and he had to fight the urge to get inside her vehicle and check for clues she was still alive. Griff couldn't get to the crash site fast enough because his protective instinct had kicked in. There was no way Aiden would contaminate the scene. Another implication was on the table. One that said a crime had occurred.

Griff continued, "According to the spokesman at the VA, Nicholas had documented emotional difficulties when he returned home. I was able to get medical information about him with Chloe's permission. There was an issue with Nicholas requesting frequent refills of his pain medications. His sister said he'd been doing better recently, and his doctor confirmed her assessment."

"Did Chloe say what she believed happened to her brother and why he'd write the note?"

"She asked for a homicide investigation."

"Murder?" Now that got Aiden's attention.

"That's the card she threw on the table."

"Do you believe her?"

"My opinion doesn't factor in. I have to follow the evidence and right now that has led to suicide..." Aiden picked up on the hesitation in Griff's voice. He may not have spent time with his cousin over the past few years but they had the kind of relationship where they could pick right up where they'd left off. People didn't change at the core of who they were.

"But now?"

"I have questions about what really happened. A few details from the case have bothered me, things I can't discuss." Griff apologized but Aiden understood the reasoning. "First things first, I need to examine the scene of the accident."

"It would be strange for her brother to commit suicide and then something random happen to her." Although, hearing the possibility hit harder than it should, considering they hadn't spoken in ten years. He chalked it up to nostalgia.

"Coincidences can happen. Life is filled with them." True enough. Aiden had experienced it plenty of times. Like the time when he showed up to his favorite fishing spot at Goldminer's Pass and ran into the same bear three times. Then again, maybe Aiden wasn't the only one who liked fishing.

Aiden walked over to the deer and examined it. There was no way he would put his prints all over a potential crime scene and he was careful when he walked so as not to trample any possible evidence.

"I see lights ahead. I'm almost to you." A few moments later, Griff's service SUV came into full view as he pulled alongside Aiden. His window was down. "Mind helping me put some cones out to block off the road?"

"Not at all." The two embraced in a bear hug the minute Griff exited his vehicle.

"Good to see you, Aiden." The sentiment was returned. They both seemed content to leave it at that.

Aiden followed Griff to the back of his vehicle where he pulled out bright orange cones and handed a stack over. "I'll take this side if you want to block off the other side of the street so no one can drive through. Careful where you walk."

Aiden accepted the offering thinking how right it felt to see his cousin again even if being back in Gunner had him slightly off-kilter. He walked along the gravel shoulder and toward the opposite side where the deer lie, hating to see an animal's life end this way.

One-by-one, he placed the cones in a line blocking access to the small highway. This wasn't the homecoming he'd anticipated but it was good to see Griff.

Watching as his cousin put on a pair of gloves, Aiden moved back to the SUV. Griff picked up the purse in the floor of the passenger side and set it on the driver's seat. With two fingers, he extracted a brown wallet. "Let's see what we have here."

The snap came undone easily. There was an ID in a holder and slots for credit cards. Griff studied the ID. He shot an apologetic look toward Aiden. "It's hers. It belongs to Chloe. And there's cash in here." He flipped through the bills. "I'd say about a hundred dollars."

"That rules out being robbed." Aiden wasn't quite ready for the gut punch that accompanied hearing the news.

"Where is she then?" His mind snapped to abduction and a few other horrible scenarios. He pushed those unproductive thoughts aside. There was a possible connection between her brother's case and her going missing, if that's what had happened here. Other unwanted thoughts joined in. He thought of search parties dredging through the woods, K-9 sniffers being deployed all with the hope of finding Chloe while the mission was search and rescue and not recovery.

Aiden turned on the flashlight app on his phone. While Griff inspected the contents of her purse and vehicle, he checked out the scene. The position of the deer had been bothering him and the location of impact.

Granted, a deer could do a lot of damage to a vehicle. Headlights blinded them and the animals never knew what had hit them. A driver might not see one until it was too late to stop. This kind of thing happened more often that it should, a reality of living in the country. Colorado roads could be even worse, especially coming down the mountain from Aiden's favorite fishing spot at Goldminer's Pass. Even driving slowly wasn't a guarantee that a deer wouldn't leap in front of his truck last minute.

Aiden shined his light on the deer, scanning its body for signs of foul play. A deer on the side of the road could be a convenient reason for a crash. Where did that leave Chloe? Following down the hit-a-deer scenario, he figured she could've been hurt and maybe decided to go for help. The first question that came to mind; why wouldn't she use her cell phone?

Cell service could be spotty in these parts. He checked his own for bars. He had one. If she was on a different carrier she might not have had any, but it was safe to assume there was cell coverage out there. His call to Griff had proved it.

But, say she didn't have the same carrier and didn't have service. Wouldn't she walk toward town? Wouldn't he have passed her on the road? Not if she'd been picked up by a Good Samaritan. If she had, wouldn't Griff have been notified about the accident?

What if she was hurt? She could've banged her head on any number of places. Head injuries could be tricky and she could be walking around in the woods, lost, an easy meal for a male black bear at night. He wondered if she still kicked her shoes off when she drove. He moved to the driver's side where Griff had been moments before. His cousin had moved onto the backseat, using his flashlight to search for evidence.

The dome light lit the seats and part of the dashboard but it was hard to see anything on the floor. A flash of hot pink caught his attention. He shined his phone's light under the seat. Her flip-flops had been kicked off and placed on the floorboard, half-tucked underneath her seat just like she used to do in high school. *Old habits die hard*, he thought.

"What is it?" Griff asked. "What did you find?"

"Her shoes. They're right here." He knew better than to touch them. Instead, he stepped back and let Griff take a closer look as he tried not to focus on what that meant for Chloe. He'd heard about criminals who caused an accident and then robbed the confused and sometimes disoriented driver. Until recent events, he wouldn't have thought that possible in a town like Gunner. Considering the crime wave his hometown had been enduring, he was starting to think no town was immune.

Griff lifted his gaze to scan the area.

"You think she's out there? Hurt? Lost?" A scenario ran through Aiden's mind that involved Chloe on the run from would-be robbers and getting lost in the woods. Of course, that didn't explain her purse and its contents being left intact.

Griff held up a cell phone using his finger and thumb. "This belongs to her."

A robber would've taken something. Money. Cell phone. Credit cards. A criminal wouldn't leave them in place in her purse. Hell, it would've been easy to snatch the whole thing and run, which bothered him. The thought she could've gotten herself involved in something illegal wasn't a serious consideration. She'd always walked the straight and narrow. As far as Aiden knew, Nicholas did the same.

Phoenix had told Aiden about asking their father if Nicholas could stay at Casa Grande senior year after Chloe had asked Phoenix to watch out for her brother. She'd offered to move out of the dorm, even though she was required to live there freshman year, and find an apartment for the two of them. She'd promised Nicholas that she'd figure out a way to work out their living arrangements even though it would mean her cutting back on classes and taking a job. Nicholas had refused and said he'd sleep outside before he'd let her make the sacrifice. Phoenix had reasoned that several of his brothers had moved out and there was plenty of room on the ranch. T.J. had shot down the idea. So, Aiden had reached out to Dakota, who'd slipped the high schooler in the bunkhouse for a few nights until a buddy's family stepped up.

T.J. had been hard on his sons. Rumor had it that losing his wife had caused him to harden toward the world and even his own flesh and blood couldn't bring him back. He'd buried himself in his work and hired Marianne to take care of his children.

Aiden couldn't imagine loving someone to the degree he'd become consumed by the person to the point losing them would break him. The only time he'd come close to caring for someone to that degree was high school, was Chloe. That was a long time ago. And he'd been smart enough to catch himself before he'd fallen into that trap with her.

Eyes searching the ground, Aiden walked the perimeter of the vehicle. Supposing Chloe did hit the deer, as unlikely as that was beginning to seem, wouldn't she investigate? He closed his eyes for a second and imagined her getting out of the driver's seat. She might be in shock and that could be the reason she'd left the door wide open. She also might've believed she was coming right back. She could've gotten out to try to help the deer. That seemed like something she would've done. And then she might check her own vehicle to see how badly that was damaged.

And then what? She could've made her way to the deer and realized there was no way to help. Hitting any living creature would traumatize the Chloe he used to know. She had the kindest heart of anyone he'd met but that didn't mean she was a doormat. She had the kind of fire that matched the red streaks in her wavy auburn hair.

How many times had she joked her hair color was meant to be a warning? More times than he could count and yet it had always made him smile every time she said it.

Spending time with Chloe had always been easy. She'd almost make him forget the hell he faced at home if he stepped an inch out of line.

No matter how many times Aiden went over this scenario in his head, it still didn't end with her missing. Say she freaked out after hitting the deer. Wouldn't she go back to her vehicle? At least search for a signal on her phone? Walking away willingly from her purse, her wallet with money inside, and her cell made no sense.

"Why would she leave the scene?" he asked his cousin. Griff might have ideas that Aiden hadn't thought about.

"I can't work it out in my mind, either." Griff rounded the back of her vehicle. He'd retrieved a floodlight from his service vehicle and was shining it on the ground next to her door. "I'm guessing you've run through the scenario of a head injury."

"Airbags, right. They've obviously deployed. Not a surprise if she really hit that deer. So, why would she have hit her head?"

"Hold on a sec. What do you mean *if*?"

Aiden turned and walked to the deer. Even before Griff made it next to him, he said, "I see what you mean."

"I'm no physicist but if she swerved to miss the deer and made contact here." He pointed toward the sizable dent in the front driver's side of her SUV. "Would the animal actually be lying like this?"

Griff moved the beam of light around and seemed to catch onto something. Aiden followed him to the other side of the deer.

"See that?" Griff moved the light in a trail from the deer to the pavement about twenty feet away.

Aiden bent closer and followed the trail, nodding his head. "The buck was dragged and someone tried to cover the fact by kicking gravel around."

"Why would someone do that?" Griff's question was rhetorical. He stood there, retracing the trail.

"The obvious reason is the deer was a convenient excuse for the crash. Maybe someone was trying to cover up the fact that they hit her." Aiden moved to the SUV again and examined the dents. "Can you come here and shine the big light?"

Griff did. "This has been wiped clean."

"The other parts of her SUV are dirty." A horrible thought crossed Aiden's mind. One he didn't want to consider but couldn't ignore. Was it possible that Chloe had been murdered like her brother, and the scene was set up to look like an accident while her brother's was meant to look like suicide? Those explanations were easy enough to believe. The unfortunate Brighton family...so much tragedy. Had someone dragged her out of her vehicle and into the woods? Or had she fought back and ran? Was she out there somewhere, alone, in the night? Hurt? Bleeding? The word *helpless* and Chloe didn't belong in the same sentence. But, if she'd been surprised, attacked or hurt in some way she could be out there defenseless.

"I'll call it in and get every available person on the hunt." Griff must've made similar assumptions. It was logical thinking and yet Aiden prayed it wasn't true. Chloe Brighton had been through more than enough for one lifetime. She deserved a break. *Brighton?* Was that still her last name? Aiden realized he'd just assumed she was still single. Hell, even his brothers were settling down like there was no tomorrow. Aiden, and Eli, the oldest, were the only two bachelors left. Eli had two children and a socialite ex who'd abandoned the family after the birth of their daughter.

Aiden shook his head. He had no intention of settling down and yet he couldn't imagine a person who would be capable of walking out on his or her own flesh and blood. Quinns weren't built that way. For all T.J.'s faults, and there'd been plenty, he'd stuck around.

Moving to the woods opposite Chloe's vehicle, Aiden shouted her name. He walked in a little deeper and listened. Croaks and chirps typical of the woods at night were all that answered. He shone his small light, but he was unable to see more than five feet in front of him. He called out to Chloe again. If she was there, he hoped she could hear him. He needed her to know that help was on the way.

All the shouting might be for nothing if she'd been abducted, because that was another glaring possibility. One he didn't want to consider. Aiden overheard Griff talking to one of his deputies, explaining that Chloe Brighton's vehicle had been in an accident and she might be in trouble. He'd said *Brighton*. The fact she was still single caused his chest to squeeze. He wrote it off as muscle memory. She'd been his best friend and first love, and had left a mark on his heart.

Aiden called Cayden, who picked up on the first ring.

"Hello?" His brother sounded groggy, like he'd just fallen asleep.

"Sorry to wake you. On my way home, I came across a situation on the highway—"

"Is everything all right? Are you okay?" Cayden's voice now sounded like he'd just downed a shot of espresso.

"I'm fine. Do you remember Chloe Brighton?"

"From high school?" A yawn came through the line. Cayden lowered his voice when he said, "Everything's good. It's my brother, Aiden. You can go back to sleep." His brother had found true happiness. He and his fiancée were expecting a child soon. Cayden returned to the call. "Go ahead."

"Yes, that's the one. Her vehicle is abandoned on the highway. She might be in the woods, lost, possibly injured. I was thinking we could rally the troops and set up a search party. Griff is calling in his deputies and I just heard him rounding up the volunteer fire department."

"This sounds serious. How far from Quinnland are you?"

"Not far. I was less than twenty minutes from home."

"I'll gather up the others and be right there." He could hear shuffling noises, like his brother was already getting out of bed.

"Thanks, man. And bring as many flashlights as you can find." Aiden ended the call without asking whether or not his brother planned to bring T.J. into the picture. All the mess with his father could be dealt with later and Aiden would take all the help he could get in the search for Chloe. He turned to his cousin. "Can I borrow that floodlight?"

"Maybe you should wait until a search team arrives. We have no idea what we're dealing with out there and no one should go in alone." As much as Aiden wanted to argue, his cousin was right. Going in by himself could be dangerous and especially since he didn't have a weapon.

Minutes ticked by as he paced on the shoulder while Griff busied himself placing pieces of evidence into paper bags. He started snapping pictures of the scene.

The knot that had formed in Aiden's gut tightened as he thought about what might have happened to Chloe. Where could she be and what had truly happened here?

Nothing was adding up. The longer he stood there, the more danger she could be in. The image of his former best friend trying to fend off a bear or wild hog assaulted him.

Aiden started pacing as more of those pictures haunted him. No. He couldn't let himself dwell on a scenario that meant Chloe was dead.

3

I t didn't take long for a set of headlights to approach from the deer side of the highway. The cell in his hand buzzed. He checked the screen and saw a text from his brother, Liam, stating they'd arrived.

Gravel crunched underneath the truck's tires as Aiden bolted toward the lights. From behind him, other vehicles started pulling up, no doubt deputies and everyone who could be rounded up.

The doors of the king cab truck opened, and Eli, Isaac, Liam, Noah, and Cayden exited. Ranch foreman and longtime family friend, Dakota Viera, moved slowly out of the driver's seat. Aiden watched, waited—hoped?—for another person to exit the vehicle.

Out of the blue, a stab of disappointment pierced Aiden that his father wasn't with them. He dismissed the feeling as being overly sentimental.

"It's good to see you guys." One-by-one, he bear hugged the men he'd been closest to his entire childhood and knew he could count on in a heartbeat if he needed help like tonight. Nothing had changed. Quinns would always have each other's backs. "Griff is probably briefing his deputies, so we might want to jog over there and listen in."

Seeing his family together again struck him in a place he didn't realize existed anymore.

"Phoenix is in Austin. We figured we brought enough help and would find her before he could make the drive." As he watched, a handful of ranch hands pulled up in a truck and parked behind Dakota. They'd assembled quite a team on short notice.

"I appreciate you guys coming here." The group hurried over to Griff, where he was briefing his deputies.

Griff acknowledged his family with a nod. "Does everyone here know Chloe or remember what she looks like?"

Most heads nodded, a few of the ranch hands shook theirs.

"Deputy Sayer, can you pull up a picture of Chloe Brighton from her social media account for anyone who needs it?"

"On it, boss." Sayer pulled out an electronic pad and tapped a few times. "Everyone who needs to see, come on over."

A couple of the workers tucked their balled fists into their jean pockets and headed over. In the last half hour, clouds had rolled in and the threat of rain hung heavy in the air. A bolt of lightning raced across the sky, lighting the velvet blue canopy. Aiden didn't need rain to complicate matters.

"Here's what I'm thinking," Griff started as a vehicle roared up and parked. Jefferson Collier stepped out and made a beeline for Griff.

"What happened to my cousin?" His demand for an answer was met by a calm headshake from Griff.

"That's what we're trying to figure out—"

"She won't be found standing around here talking." Jefferson stomped toward Chloe's SUV and was backed away by Deputy Sayer.

Aiden couldn't help thinking that causing a disruption that slowed down the process wasn't the guy's smartest move, no matter how concerned the man was.

"If you want to be part of this, pipe down." Griff didn't hide his annoyance. He shot a glare toward Jefferson, who put his hands up. "Like I was saying, we fan out and move together. Keeping close ensures everyone's safety and is the best way to canvas the area and get the best coverage. Everybody okay to get started?"

"Yes," came from the collective voices.

"Deputy Poncho will remain here at the vehicles to ensure safety." He looked to Poncho, who nodded and frowned, clearly preferring to be in the action rather than assigned to babysit cars. "Is Kellerman on his way with the tow truck?"

"Yes, sir," came Poncho's response.

Having an SUV and a deer blocking the two-lane highway was probably a hazard, but all Aiden could think about was finding Chloe.

Eli walked over and put his arm around Aiden's shoulders as the two made their way to the line being formed on the side of the road. "We'll find her, bro."

Flashlights were doled out. Since one side of the highway was fenced off, they started opposite, to the east. With a dozen-and-a-half men, the group fanned out pretty wide. Words couldn't express how much it meant to Aiden to have his brothers show up on a dime.

There'd been good memories growing up on the ranch. All of which involved these men. The seven of them had been a tight-knit bunch. Add in five cousins and they'd made quite a group. Some of their teachers might've classified them as a handful. A smile crept across Aiden's face despite his somber mood. Looking at his brothers now, they seemed at peace. How they'd found it in their hearts to forgive T.J. was beyond him. Maybe there was some kind of magic in the water at the ranch that erased the past.

As the men formed a line facing the woods, Cayden backtracked to the SUV. Aiden followed his brother, who used to track poachers for a living before his—very pregnant—fiancée.

Cayden flashed his light on the patch of road next to the driver's door. He crouched low and shined the light underneath her vehicle. He popped to his feet and rounded the other side of the SUV. Aiden followed as his brother trailed a line toward the woods. The others had already broken through the trees. Occasional lights flickered here and there, shining light through an otherwise pitch-black night.

Cayden stood on the edge of the tree line. Aiden could tell his brother's mind was working through possibilities. And then like a hound on a scent, he moved with purpose, motioning for Aiden to follow.

Aiden kept pace, spreading out and flooding the underbrush with light as he listened for any signs of life. A chorus of insects filled his ears but there was no sign of a human. He must've been searching for a solid half hour before he heard the first promising sound. Heart in his throat, he moved to the left approximately ten feet and toward a large mesquite tree.

Crouching low on his haunches, he checked the underbrush near the tree. Nothing. So, he moved closer. He examined the tree and caught sight of something. His inspection revealed a red spot—blood?—and a piece of long hair. *Chloe's?*

The strand was dark. *Auburn?*

Could this belong to her? The likelihood some random person was out here in the woods and had left this behind in the past twenty-four hours was unlikely. This *had* to be a find and their first break.

A shot of adrenaline coursed through him as he pulled out his phone and tucked the flashlight underneath his arm. With one hand, he took a picture of the strand of hair and then sent it to Griff.

He listened for sounds that others in the search party were nearby and got confirmation when he heard footsteps crunching through the underbrush. Someone to his left was whistling a low tune as he searched.

The response from Griff was immediate. *Where are you?*

Good question. He couldn't pinpoint the exact location and he'd separated enough from Cayden not have him in his sights anymore. The best he could do was tell Griff who he'd been with when they'd started out. *I'm with Cayden.*

His cell buzzed, indicating a call. It was Griff.

"I'm trying to make my way east toward your position," Griff said.

"So far, all I've seen is a hair and possibly some blood on the tree. There are no other signs of her." The fact that there could be blood on the tree meant she could be lying somewhere unconscious. Even if he called out to her, she might not be able to hear him or wake up enough to respond. Even so, it was worth a try. He moved the phone away from his mouth and called her name. All he heard in response was more of that whistling. So, he tried again a little louder this time.

Nothing.

He put the phone back to his ear. "I don't want to dash your hopes, but if she was here she might not still be."

Griff didn't say this was the first hope that they'd had so far in finding her and Aiden appreciated him for it. "It's a start."

Still on his haunches, Aiden moved at a slow and steady pace. He was abruptly stopped by the sound of a low growl. He froze.

In the manner of seconds, his brother, Cayden, was at his side. An experienced tracker was a good thing to have in a search and rescue mission. Cayden's movements were so stealth that Aiden hardly knew he was there.

Aiden brought his index finger up to his lips after making eye contact with his brother. He nodded in the direction of the growls. Cayden tilted his head and listened. A deep, throaty growl came from a bush straight ahead. It had the sound of a wolf and was either frightened or threatened. Neither of which would bode well for Aiden and his brother if one of them made a wrong or sudden move.

And then he heard it. One word. Human. "Help."

The voice was faint but unmistakably belonged to a female. The low growls intensified as Aiden came into contact with two black eyes and a show of white teeth. The animal was in the brush next to Chloe —it had to be her.

"You're okay," Aiden soothed the animal.

Cayden froze. Sudden movement could spook the animal into a bite. They'd grown up on a ranch and had more wild animal encounters and close calls between them than Aiden cared to count.

"Zeus. No." It sounded like it took great effort to get out those two words out, but they had an instant effect on the dog. Leaves on the scrub bush shook and then a hand emerged. Aiden took it, noticing how small it was in comparison to his. The grip was strong as she latched onto his wrist and pulled herself toward him.

"It's okay, Zeus." The frail voice was barely more than a whisper and nothing like he remembered Chloe's to be.

"I'm just here to help, Zeus. I'm not going to hurt anyone." Aiden kept his voice as quiet and soothing as he could, knowing that animals picked up on emotion. They also were masters at picking up the scent of fear and adrenaline. So, Aiden did his best to radiate a sense of calm.

Somewhere in the background, Cayden was making a call to Griff, informing him of who they'd found and giving their location as best as he could. Cayden was able to give coordinates and Aiden realized his brother was used to working in these conditions. Cayden also relayed the news of a scared and possibly injured dog on the scene.

The second Chloe cleared the bush and got a good look at Aiden, she threw her arms around his neck.

"Aiden." For a second, everything righted itself in the world and he had the feeling he'd come home.

"We're going to get you to safety, Chloe." He could feel her nodding against his neck, but she basically curled her body around him as he lifted her.

"Hold on." Cayden shined his light on her bare feet and then her legs, scanning her for injuries.

"My head. Hurts."

"Medical help is waiting as soon as we get out of these woods." Aiden's reassurance was met with a nod.

"Zeus. My... Zeus." She sounded tired, but her words weren't slurred. That was a good sign.

"Do you mind checking on her dog?" Aiden asked his brother. Cayden had plenty of experience dealing with animals having grown up on a ranch.

"Zeus," Chloe called. A beautiful German shepherd emerged. Aiden wasted no time setting out toward the highway with Chloe secured in his arms and his brother leading the way. It was difficult to assess her true injuries, but he had to get her out of there and to medical treatment.

The second break came when Zeus followed. But Aiden didn't

look back. Urgency built inside him the tighter her grip around his neck became. Was she struggling to stay conscious? He whispered soothing words to let her know that she was okay now, and he meant them as he followed his brother. Come hell or high water, Aiden planned to deliver on the promise he made that he wouldn't let anything else happen to her.

After walking for what felt like an eternity, he caught sight of bright lights ahead. "We're almost there, Chloe. Hang on for me a little bit longer."

And that's when her body went limp.

"No. No. No. Wake up, Chloe. I need you to wake up. Stay with me. We're almost there." He tamped down the rising panic as he focused on the last twenty feet of their journey.

Cayden was already shouting for help. "Over here. I have an injured woman. She needs help."

Aiden's thighs burned and his arms felt like they would fall off, but he pushed himself to run faster. As he neared the clearing, a pair of EMTs came running toward him.

"Is she breathing?" One of the EMTs asked. She had black hair and olive skin. She wasn't much bigger than the woman in his arms. And she seemed familiar. The name came to him. Sheila Stillwater.

"I can't tell for certain." His response came through labored breaths. The time to figure out who everyone was and remember how he knew them would come later. Much to his surprise, Zeus darted past him and toward Chloe's SUV. Aiden stopped as Sheila checked Chloe's pulse.

Sheila counted and then glanced at him as her partner came running toward them with a gurney. "It's strong. What do you know about her injuries?"

"Not much. She mentioned her head hurt. Her feet are bitten and swollen. She was barefoot. She was conscious enough to say the dog's name."

"Zeus." Sheila flashed her eyes at him. "I know Chloe's brother. Zeus belonged to him."

Seeing Sheila's familiar face must've been the reason the dog had taken off towards the sport utility vehicle. "Chloe seemed aware of what was going on at first. We got close to you and her body went limp."

"Okay, we'll take it from here." Sheila motioned toward a male EMT who was about a foot and a half shorter than Aiden.

"Tell me where you want her."

Sheila motioned toward the gurney. Her partner helped Aiden position Chloe on the gurney.

"There was blood on a tree near where we found her and what I believe is a strand of her hair," he said.

"Anything else we should know?" Sheila hopped into action.

"That's all I have."

Sheila turned Chloe's head to one side as the other EMT started strapping her in. Her hair was matted at the spot near the crown of her head. Sheila slipped on gloves and parted the hair at the crown. There was a pump knot and a cut. Sheila spewed medical jargon into the radio clipped to her left shoulder. The faster she talked, the more his worry grew. Shock at seeing her in this condition, on a gurney looking so helpless, was a gut punch.

In the next moment, Chloe was being loaded into the back of the ambulance. Sheila shot a quick look toward Aiden. "You can follow us to the hospital."

And then the doors closed. Aiden took a couple of steps away from the vehicle, still in complete shock at what had transpired since returning to Gunner. He could scarcely process everything that had just happened. His mind had snapped out of the road trip fog darn fast and all he could think about was Chloe's safety. She needed to be okay. More than okay. Seeing her again had stirred feelings he'd tucked away long ago when he put Gunner, and her, in the rearview mirror.

Now, everything he'd tried to walk away from came roaring back and an ache formed in his chest. There'd been too many times that he'd wanted to call her and find out how she was doing. Logic had always won out. What would he have said to her? The thought of reducing their bond to an occasional 'check-in' phone call had felt like minimizing what they'd shared.

It had seemed easier to redirect his thoughts to something more productive rather than miss her. And he had missed her more than he wanted to admit.

In his peripheral, he saw Zeus curled up in the back seat of Chloe's SUV. Cayden stood sentinel next to the opened door as Griff and the others started filing in.

Before Aiden could take off and for reasons he couldn't explain, he needed to check on the animal. Approaching his brother, he asked, "How is he?"

"Hurt. But he won't let me get close enough to assess his injuries. I put in a call to Michael and he's on his way. He's a good dog. And based on the dog tags that he's wearing, he was a soldier. He deserves and will get the best treatment."

Aiden pulled his brother into a bear hug. "I have to go now. Thank the others for me and tell them I'll be home as soon as I can."

"You're not going to the hospital by yourself. Noah is taking the first shift with you and the others have worked out the rest. I'll be along after I make sure this guy is in good hands," he motioned toward Zeus, "and then go home and check on my wife. You don't have to do any of this alone, bro."

It had been a really long time since Aiden had heard those words. It was in that moment that he realized how much he missed home.

4

"You want me to drive?"

Aiden was caught off guard by Noah's question. He turned and found himself in the middle of an enthusiastic bear hug.

"It's good to see you, bro." Aiden started toward his truck as he fished keys out of his pocket and then pitched them toward his brother. "My hands were glued to the steering wheel for more than fifteen hours straight. I'll take you up on your offer."

Road fatigue had been replaced by adrenaline for the past few hours since finding Chloe's SUV, but that would fade and exhaustion would take its place.

Noah took the driver's seat. Since pretty much all the Quinn brothers were similar in height, Noah didn't have to do a lot to adjust the seat or the mirrors.

The fifteen-hour straight drive had left him tired. Too much sitting. Too much traffic that had thickened the longer he drove. Not enough patience, which ran in short supply sometime after hour fourteen.

"Congratulations, brother. Sorry I didn't make the wedding."

Being so far away, it had been easy to ignore the fact that he missed his brothers.

"You had your reasons. No one has ever doubted how much you care for any one of us, T.J. aside."

"Can I ask a question?"

"Go ahead. I'm an open book." Noah had always been upfront, honest.

"Why did you stay, Noah? I mean, you could have gone anywhere, done anything. Few people are smarter than you. You chose to stay at the ranch and I guess I never understood the decision." Aiden couldn't fathom making that same choice.

"I didn't like him any more than anyone else did." Noah shrugged a shoulder like it was no big deal. He let his right wrist rest on top of the steering wheel as he drove. "Where would I go? I love Texas, so moving out of state would be out of the question. More than that, our land is a part of me. I guess that sounds kind of corny but it's true. I can't imagine living anywhere else and I want my family to grow up there."

"Are you and Mikayla expecting?" It was a legitimate question. It seemed there'd been a baby boom on the ranch recently.

"Not us. We're not in any rush to start that part of our lives." Noah's voice had a hint of something. Sadness? Regret? "How about you?"

"Don't look at me. Work keeps me too busy to date enough to get serious with anyone." Aiden took note that his brother had turned the tables real quick. He decided to go with the flow. "Now that we're all here...any idea what the big secret is? What's so important that T.J. needs all seven of us under one roof before he'll talk?"

"No doubt you've heard the rumor about him being sick. But we'll have to wait because he's not home right now." Noah didn't break focus on the stretch of road in front of them.

"I guess I can stick around a few days. Any idea where he is and why?" Aiden heard the bitterness in his own tone. Too many years of suppressed anger, he figured. Bottling his emotions hadn't done him a whole helluva lot of good so far. In fact, it had made him angry and he was beginning to see that was as productive as using gasoline to douse a forest fire.

"He's in Dallas. Cayden's best guess is that he's there for some kind of treatment. He's under the impression that Pop won't be home for a little while. He asked about Madison's pregnancy and Cayden was under the impression that Pop didn't want to miss the birth."

"When is she due?"

"A couple weeks, give or take. I don't know that much about pregnancies and birthing babies, but her doctor said something about the fact that she was dilating. He also said these things can be unpredictable and no two births are the same. Having said that, he didn't think there would be a rush. She has to come back every week to be checked out and is supposed to call if she has any signs of labor."

"Sounds like she could go at any minute." Aiden didn't know much about those things, either. He tried to stay away from all those terms, mother, baby. The last thing he needed in his life was a wife or child. His business was booming, and he couldn't imagine slowing down.

"Her doctor seems to think she has a little more time, but he said it was almost impossible to gauge these things and that these little babies seem to like to prove him wrong a lot."

"Sounds risky to leave right now. And it doesn't sound like T.J. dropped any hints as to why he was going to Dallas."

"Nope. That's the sixty-four-million-dollar question. Even Eli decided doctor appointments or some kind of medical treatment might be involved. I personally have no idea. He looks older to me all of a sudden but it could just be that I wasn't paying much attention before."

"I wish someone had bothered to tell me he wasn't around." He heard the grumpiness in his own voice and put his hand up. "That was out of line."

Noah's response was simple. "We didn't know you were coming."

"Fair point." Aiden got himself in check. "Sorry for sounding like a jerk. It's been a long time since I set foot in Gunner."

Noah didn't say *too long* even though the words hung in the air.

Aiden knew it wasn't a judgment. The Quinn brothers had always been a tight-knit bunch growing up. As adults, most had gone their separate ways, which didn't mean they didn't still love each other.

During the rest of the ride to the hospital, Aiden and his brother fell into an easy routine of talking about childhood memories and teasing each other. Aiden hadn't felt this kind of ease in a long time. Even he was beginning to wonder why he'd stayed out of contact for so long.

Noah parked in the lot and accompanied Aiden into the lobby. He gave their names to the attendant and her eyes glittered when she heard *Quinn*. His last name was not something that he'd been proud of in a long time. His only connection to Quinnland Ranch was his brothers. It was starting to dawn on him just how much he missed having those guys around and how lonely it had been without them. His stubbornness had held him back too long.

"Chloe Brighton isn't allowed visitors right now," the night attendant said.

"Do you have a cafeteria or a place where we can get a decent cup of coffee?"

The woman behind the information desk smiled. "That'll be just on the other side of the lobby in the vending machine. Not sure how good the coffee is, but it's strong."

"Perfect." Noah returned the smile and thanked her. He and Aiden walked side-by-side across the expansive lobby and down the hall.

A row of vending machines lined the wall. Noah located the coffee first. He turned to Aiden. "How do you take yours?"

"Black, no sugar."

Noah gave a quick nod of approval. It occurred to Aiden as he watched his brother program in the second cup that this was the middle of the night for someone who worked on a ranch. Aiden felt compelled to make sure his brother knew he didn't have to stick around.

"Before you finish that order, I don't want to keep you out all night when you have to get up in a few hours for work."

Noah waved him off like it was nothing. It was something, though. And it meant more to Aiden than he could express.

Familiar voices floated across the room as they returned to the lobby. Griff and Eli met them halfway.

"Can't say the coffee is fresh or good, but it is lukewarm and strong if you'd like a cup," Noah said to the others. His assessment wasn't too far off base.

Eli brought Aiden into a hug. "I'll take some of that coffee. Point me in a direction."

Aiden did.

Eli turned to Griff. "You want a cup?"

"Lukewarm and strong are right up my alley. Thank you." Griff motioned toward a cluster of chairs around a small table off to the side of the lobby.

"The person at the information desk said no visitors for Chloe right now," Aiden informed Griff as they took seats. Eli joined them a moment later, handing over one of the cups. Having his family around helped ease some of his feelings of helplessness—feelings that had been tucked away for more than two decades and he was certain reached back to losing his mother at a young age. Then there was T.J. Don't even get Aiden started on his father's inability to cope with tragedy. He'd practically invented the notion of tucking away feelings and powering through.

Griff took the offering and thanked his cousin. Then, he immediately shot a cautionary look. "This conversation is off the books. Unofficial."

Heads nodded in unison.

"What do you guys know about Jefferson Collier?" Griff took a sip from his cup, and then made a face. "Not sure I'd even call that coffee, but it is lukewarm."

A collective chuckle echoed in the lobby, breaking up some of the heavy tension.

Aiden spoke first. "I know a little about him because you guys know that Chloe and I used to be close. He and Nicholas seem to have an on-again off-again friendship back in the day. She was never too thrilled when their relationship was on, saying that she didn't think Jefferson was the best person for her brother to be around."

Griff cocked an eyebrow. "Did she ever say why?"

Aiden shook his head. "It didn't come up a lot. When it did, she thought Nicholas always seemed to get the short end of the stick, whereas Jefferson came out smelling like a rose when the two got in trouble. I guess I should've asked more questions; I was a lot in my own head back then." He paused for a beat, thinking about how much he'd missed in his brothers' lives recently. Guilt penetrated his usually-thick armor. "Still am, but I'm a work in progress on that one."

To their credit, neither his brothers nor his cousin razzed him about his absence. Instead, this last statement was met with nods of acceptance. In the past, those words would've been insincere, foreign. This felt on the right track to Aiden and he allowed a little peek of light into the dark corners of his heart. In shutting out his father, he'd pushed everyone away. That was about to change.

"Why don't you like him?" Eli asked.

Griff shrugged. "Anytime there's a search for a missing person, the first people I look at are the ones who show up to a search party. Jefferson Collier was one of them. You saw him."

No one could've missed the show he put on.

"Off to the side, before the search party hit the woods, he said that he wanted me to know he was always available if I needed more help."

"Oh. That almost sounds like he wasn't expecting us to find her." Aiden took another sip of his brew. The taste was strong, and he didn't mind the bitterness.

"We may not have without Cayden and Zeus." Griff shifted his gaze to Aiden. "From what I gathered, he basically led you to her according to your statement."

"That's right." Aiden couldn't be more grateful for that miracle.

"I don't think he counted on the dog." Griff leaned forward, placing his elbows on top of his thighs. "If Nicholas is gone and something happens to Chloe, Jefferson might stand to inherit their land and family home. During the course of my investigation into Nicholas's disappearance, I found out from Hattie Blankenship that he made a trip to the library to ask about how inheritance worked. She said she had a stack of books he could read but he didn't want to take them. He just wanted to know what her thoughts were."

Hattie had been running the town's library since before Aiden was born. "Sounds pretty suspect if you ask me."

"He's definitely someone I'm keeping my eye on. There are a few points about Nicholas's death that haven't been sitting right with me. I recently found out he'd been talking to a guy in Austin by the name of Levi Amon, who is connected to a known anti-government group. Even with all the technology we have available to us, it's been difficult to keep a finger on that group's headquarters. Amon moves it to a new location every few weeks. He's twenty-four-years-old, angry after receiving a dishonorable discharge from the Army. He's one of those conspiracy theory guys who is considered dangerous. Those two had planned to meet up a week before Nicholas's death."

"Any idea what that was about?"

"Amon isn't really the type to give himself away. Their conversation via text was very nondescript. An alphabet letter agency has him on a watchlist." To Aiden's thinking, that meant one thing. Terror. And an alphabet letter agency most likely meant CIA.

"So a guy who doesn't like the government reaches out to a guy who came home broken, by his own account, by said government. Is that about right?" Aiden asked.

Griff nodded.

"It's probably just my imagination running wild, but is it possible Amon gave something to Nicholas that he decided he wanted back? Following that thinking, is it then possible that Nicholas denied Amon, and he somehow thinks Chloe might know the location?" Aiden called on his childhood years of having a sheriff for an uncle in his assessment. He'd overheard enough stories to be decent at piecing clues together.

"That line of thinking is on the table." Griff set his cup on the round marble table in between them. "There was another suspicious person that I discovered when Chloe handed over Nicholas's laptop. He'd been talking online to a person believed to be a woman, but we've uncovered evidence that leads us to the conclusion he's a man posing as a FoxyLady1234."

"What would the motive for murder be?"

"That's a good question because normally this sort of crime would fall into the category of robbery. Whoever got to Nicholas had to have gotten past Zeus." Griff clasped his hands together.

Aiden held his hand up, palm out. "I hear what you're saying. But this leads me to believe Nicholas would have had to have known the person who murdered him. If, in fact, he was murdered."

5

The door to the lobby opened and the doctor walked in. He was on the young side with serious eyes and a runner's build.

Noah stood first and clasped hands with the doctor. "Good to see you again, Dr. Hill."

"Likewise, Noah." Dr. Hill acknowledged the others.

"I heard you were waiting out here, so I thought I'd come deliver the good news personally," Dr. Hill said to Griff. "Ms. Brighton suffered a contusion to the back of her head. I'm hoping you can help me out. The first thing she asked about when she woke was Zeus. I'm guessing you guys know who that is."

Griff nodded. "He's her brother's dog. She's caring for him now and he was with her at the time of the accident."

Aiden took note of Griff's careful use of words.

"A-ha." Dr. Hill crossed his arms over his chest as he nodded. "That makes more sense."

Hearing that Chloe was awake, talking and clear-minded enough to ask about Zeus caused a burst of hope that she would be okay in Aiden's chest.

Dr. Hill looked directly at Aiden when he said, "I've been hearing your name quite a bit. She's been asking for you."

"Is it possible for me to go see her?" Aiden wanted to continue the discussion about her case. However, seeing with his own eyes that Chloe was awake and going to be okay trumped everything else at the moment. He couldn't begin to think of home without her here.

"If I didn't agree she would probably rip out her IV and come out here." The doctor's smile and casual demeanor loosened the knot that had formed in Aiden's stomach. "Room 412."

Aiden thanked Dr. Hill before turning toward Griff, who was already nodding in the direction of the door that the doctor had come out of a few moments ago.

"I'll need to get a statement from her as soon as possible." Griff informed, but quickly added, "I'll be right there as soon as I finish getting a statement from the good doctor here."

Dr. Hill's eyebrow flew up. Aiden moved past him, figuring he could get a moment or two alone with Chloe before Griff needed to talk to her.

A quick ride up an elevator followed by a short walk down the hallway, and he tapped at her door before stepping inside. He wasn't sure what he expected to find. A lot of machines beeping? A lot of tubes running out of her arms? A frail and frightened woman? His stomach tied in a knot at the images running through his head—images that were in stark contrast to the fiery and beautiful young woman he'd grown up beside.

Instead of looking pitiful, Chloe sat up straight, hands folded on top of her lap, wide smile despite the hell she'd just gone through. His heart took a hit at seeing her again, pounding too fast against his ribs, and that deep tucked away place inside him stirred.

"First of all, thank you for saving my life. And second, I never thought I'd see Aiden Quinn anywhere near Gunner, Texas again. It's good to see you."

"Mind if I come in?" Her gaze dropped to his smirk.

"What's that all about?" She made eyes at him.

Was he that transparent? "I should've known that you'd be sitting up with a smile on your face." Seeing her again caused the knot that had formed in his stomach to move to his chest. She was brave. It was one of many things he liked about her. Her intelligence and determination were more of her best qualities. But then if he started listing things to like about Chloe Brighton, he'd be there all night.

"My head hurts."

"Is that supposed to make me feel better?" Aiden realized just how much he missed Chloe.

"When you put it like that. I guess not."

"It could've been a lot worse." He didn't want to think about how much more so if he hadn't shown when he did.

She patted the bed. "Can you stay for a minute?"

His heart shouldn't squeeze at the request. But damned if it didn't do it anyway. "I'd like that."

Careful not to accidentally sit on her leg, he eased onto the bed and turned to face her. This close, she still had the most violet eyes with gold flecks near the irises. They were like looking at spring wildflowers in Texas. His favorite time of year.

"Be serious with me, Chloe. How do you really feel?" Her long auburn hair framed an almost too beautiful face. He could've sworn she had a physical reaction to hearing him say her name. It was a flash that passed too quickly for his liking.

"I wasn't kidding about my head hurting. It feels like someone took an ax," she motioned toward the crown of her head, wincing in pain with movement, "and slammed it right here."

The doctor had said she'd suffered a contusion. Aiden had meant to ask about a concussion. However, seeing her now it didn't seem like a good question. Growing up with six brothers and five cousins on a ranch, Aiden had seen his fair share of accidents and concussions. Chloe's speech was good. Her eyes were clear. Eyes that he had no business staring into this long. He averted his gaze, lingering a second too long on those full pink lips of hers.

His hands fisted remembering the condition in which he'd found her. He flexed his fingers to ease some of the tension.

"Griff will be in soon to get your statement while it's still fresh on your mind. You don't have to tell me anything you don't want to—"

"That's the thing." She flashed those violet eyes at him. "I remember two things, no, that's not accurate. Three things. I was taking the long way home after stopping by my parent's old place. I know I had Zeus with me. Then, I remember you. I have no idea what order any of those events occurred in. Except that common sense says they happened in that exact order."

Aiden nodded. He'd revisit the question about a concussion with her doctor when she was out of earshot. "Are memories fuzzy? Or gone?"

"Gone. The doctor said it's quite normal with head trauma. Everything else checked out. I know my name, my address. I can easily recall who the president is and today's date." She paused long enough to scrape her front teeth over her bottom lip. "I asked him about Zeus."

"He's with Michael, getting the treatment he needs." Michael had been the family's vet for years.

"And he's okay?"

"As far as I know. Michael will take good care of him." Relief relaxed the stress lines on her forehead.

"I should probably have gotten one of those seatbelts at the pet store. He must've run away after what happened to my brother. I overheard someone suggest my brother let him out of the yard, but I don't believe it's possible. A neighbor eventually saw him and was able to contain him in their yard long enough for me to come pick him up." A mix of sadness and regret flashed behind her eyes. "Did you hear about Nicholas?"

"I couldn't be sorrier, Chloe. There are no words that can express my gratitude for his service to this country and for your family's sacrifice."

He meant every word.

∿

"THANK YOU, Aiden. It really means a lot to hear you say that." To Chloe, her little brother was a hero and nothing would change her opinion of him. She was even prouder of him for the way he was putting the pieces of his life back together after his service. "I already told Griff this but there's no way my brother would've taken his own life. And there's no way he could've written that note. Plus, no one can explain the blood splatter in his kitchen."

"Blood splatter?"

"There wasn't much but Griff saw it." Aiden nodded. Chloe had no idea how much Aiden and Griff had been talking about the investigation. Right now, she was torn between concern for her brother, fear for herself, and an emotion she hadn't felt in years...longing. It was strange to feel so comforted by Aiden's presence on the one hand while it also stirred a deep ache in her chest for all the things she'd been missing in her life.

"Griff is talking to the doctor and should be here soon. Did Dr. Hill say when you'll be released?"

"I know he's keeping me for observation. Looks like I'll be here overnight at the very least." She frowned.

"You don't want to be here?"

"When's the last time anyone said they had a good night of sleep in the hospital? Plus, I need to be out there, figuring out what happened to Nicholas." She'd seen enough of the inside of these types of buildings to last a lifetime since her brother's return.

"That's a really good point about sleep. If you could leave, where would you go?"

"I guess going home isn't realistic, considering Austin is a bit of a drive from here." The thought occurred to her that she had been in a car crash. She didn't remember it. However, the doctor had told her as much when he'd asked her if she remembered anything from the wreck. "How bad off is my SUV?"

"There's a pretty sizable dent in the front on the driver side. It'll probably take a couple of days to get it straightened out." This was all so surreal. First, her brother. Then, the crash. And now, Aiden. She could scarcely believe she was looking at Aiden Quinn right now. Still tall and with muscles for days. Still with those same rugged good looks. Although, he would laugh at hearing himself described that way. Still with that hint of trouble in his eyes that made him pretty much irresistible. Even delivering bad news didn't sound as awful when it came from him; he had the kind of deep masculine voice that wrapped around her, and revived places she'd closed off a long time ago. So long, in fact, she didn't think they existed anymore.

Looking up into his eyes, she realized he was studying her. "Would there be anyone in Austin at your apartment to take care of you if the doctor released you tonight and you had transportation?"

"No." It shouldn't hurt to say that word. Chloe had always prided herself on her independence and she still did. The thought of needing someone to look after her didn't sit well. She'd always been the one to keep tabs on her little brother, to check on him and make sure he was okay. She refused to accept that she'd failed the person closest to her, or that she needed help.

Aiden fished his cell phone from his pocket and then stood up to make a call.

"What are you doing, Aiden?"

"Making arrangements for you. It may feel like a slow night with someone coming in your room to check on you every few hours and listening to all this noise but tomorrow morning will come faster than you realize. You'll be released and your SUV's in the shop. You need care."

"I can do this on my own. I can figure it out."

He shot her a look. It was the one she remembered from high school that said arguing with him produced the same results as nego-tiating with a tree. Since that wouldn't get her very far, she threw her hands up. Literally. She literally threw her hands up in the air and blew out a frustrated breath.

Aiden stopped right there. "I'm not trying to overstep my bounds here. Or maybe I am. But here's the thing, I can't walk out that door and away from you not knowing what happens next. If you had someone at home who would be offended by me stepping in and giving you a hand up, that would be a different story. I wouldn't want to tread on anyone's toes. Or if you just don't want my help. That's another story. Believe me when I say that I'm not trying to offend you by helping you while you're down—"

"You're reading this the wrong way, Aiden. Or, maybe you're not. I'm frustrated. You know how well I 'do' helpless." She also knew him well enough to know he had good intentions.

He moved back to the bed and eased to sitting. "You might feel a little vulnerable right now. But, Chloe, you are far from helpless. We've been friends a long time—"

"Have we, though? Because last time I checked, friends stayed in touch with each other and didn't move away and basically cut off all contact." The words came out harsher than she'd intended but then she'd been bottling up these feelings for a long time and he needed to know where he stood now.

"All right, tough guy. What's your plan?" It was a little bit infuriating that he didn't take the bait for the argument she'd just tried to pick with him. She realized on some level that she wasn't just trying to be mean. It had just been a really long time since there was anyone around she didn't have to keep her guard up with. She'd always been able to shoot straight from the hip with Aiden. Right up until the day he'd disappeared. The conversation could take place at a later date, though. Because she needed to understand why he'd walked away from Gunner, from her.

"You know I don't do apologies." Apparently, he didn't do goodbyes, either. "I'm here now and I'd like to help if you'll allow me to."

Chloe blew out a breath. "I'm just so angry, Aiden."

"I know. You have every right to be." He seemed to know that she'd switched subjects to her brother.

"Maybe so. But it's not fair to take it out on you and especially when you're just here trying to help."

The spark returned to his eyes. "Does that mean what I think it does?"

She nodded and smiled. "I'll accept whatever help I can get. It's really good to see you, Aiden."

"I was just thinking the same thing about you." He reached over and took her hand in his and she ignored the sensual shivers that caused goosebumps to form. A dozen butterflies released in her stomach. She did her level best to ignore her body's reaction.

"So what actually brings you into town? I heard about your brothers coming back. I wasn't kidding when I said you were the last person I expected to see in Gunner." She needed to think of something besides the way his shirt outlined a broad chest. He shrugged, and the cotton of his shirt pulled and stretched over his muscles. And Aiden had muscles for days. "T.J. called a family meeting."

She couldn't hide her shock. "And you came?"

"If you know my brothers are in town then you also know about the weddings and babies."

"So, you really came for them?" That made more sense. She had no idea what had happened between him and his father but she wondered if it had been the reason he'd taken off and never looked back.

"Yes. And as it turns out, I was the last one to arrive and T.J. is holding up this announcement waiting for all of us to be together."

"Sounds serious. Is he okay?"

"That seems to be the question of the day. None of my brothers know the real reason for the meeting. Dakota and Marianne are being tightlipped."

"Which probably means they have no idea."

He rocked his head. "My thoughts exactly. Even if they knew, they wouldn't break his confidence. There's a reason both have been in his employment for decades. He trusts them more than his own children."

She picked up on something in his tone. Sadness? Regret?

"When did you get back?" She couldn't help but wonder if the two had had words.

Aiden looked at his watch and smirked.

"A couple of hours ago. And, technically, I haven't been home yet."

"Seriously?" Chloe selfishly didn't want him to leave. She chalked it up to memories of the past and missing his friendship and hoped the little voice in the back of her mind would let her get away with it and not call her out. In good conscience, she couldn't hold him up more than she already had. "Well, you have to go home."

"Funnily enough, he's not even there." That smirk resurfaced and his gaze lingered on hers. "And I'd much rather stay here."

"I'm confused." She tried to mentally shake off her physical reaction to him.

"I just found out about it myself. He won't be home for days and after a fifteen-hour drive I'm not turning tail to run back to Colorado. Let me help you, Chloe. It'll give me something to do."

She raked her teeth over her bottom lip, definitely considering his offer. On balance, what could it hurt?

"What do you have in mind, Aiden?"

There was a knock at the door and a moment of dread filled Chloe. It was an odd feeling that she didn't want to share Aiden so soon after seeing each other again. There was a sharper edge to him now. She couldn't explain except to say he had a loner quality. Granted, he'd always been his own person and had always preferred life on the fringe. He'd been dangerous to her then and even more so than now.

"Come in."

Griff walked into the room followed by Eli and Noah. Aiden started to get up. Chloe reached out to touch his arm, wanting him to stay right where he was. She acknowledged Eli and Noah, and then Griff. He asked for her statement, which didn't take long to give.

"Can you tell me what happened?" she asked. The question was directed at Griff and it got all the Quinn brothers' attention.

"Your vehicle struck or was struck by an object large enough to cause significant damage to the front end on the driver's side. A deer was hit, as well, and its location is under investigation." She raised an eyebrow at that. "There is reason to believe the deer might have been moved postmortem."

"Are you suggesting someone staged the accident?" The thought hit like a tsunami.

"Or covered up for something else."

6

"How would anyone know where she would be?" Aiden couldn't figure that part out.

"Whoever is ultimately responsible could have been watching the area. Or had a scout who phoned in a tip, much like I would use an informant. Career criminals have their own networks and their reach can be surprisingly far and deep." Griff's training and experience no doubt gave him plenty of perspective.

"Okay, that makes sense." Aiden wanted to take it from a different point of view. "What could anyone have to gain by hurting Chloe?"

Griff's gaze bounced from Aiden to Chloe. "I was kind of hoping you could tell me or send me in a direction."

"I have no idea who would want to hurt my brother or myself." She flashed her eyes at Griff. "Or why my brother is missing." She put special emphasis on that last word. "My only thought is that he knew something and now someone thinks I know something."

The look that passed between Griff and Chloe didn't go unnoticed by Aiden.

"I know we've covered this ground before," Griff started. "I'm working through the list of names of your brother's known friends and associates. Did he ever mention speaking to anyone online?"

Chloe shook her head. She shifted her gaze toward the ceiling and to the left, a sure sign that she was being honest and trying to recall information. "No. He did get upset when he was having trouble with this laptop. It seemed really important to him to have internet access. I remember having to lend him mine while his was getting looked at."

Griff's eyebrow shot up like this was the first time she'd mentioned it.

"I didn't really think about it all that much at the time. It seemed like surfing the internet was one of the few things he enjoyed in order to pass the time. He also told me that he was doing some research on prosthetics and searching out a few new workouts that he could do at home. It's all part of why I told you he was improving. He also wanted to learn how to order groceries until he could have his old Jeep modified so that he could drive it again."

Aiden had to admit that based on what she was saying it sounded like Nicholas was making plans for a future, although Aiden hadn't known Chloe's brother as well as her, he'd been around him when they were all kids. Plus, he was certainly no expert on mental health so his thoughts came with a grain of salt, but Nicholas's disappearance was just that. A disappearance. Until a body was found, there was no way Griff could classify this as a death, suicide or otherwise. For all anyone knew, one of his buddies could've picked him up. A suicide note and blood splatter were circumstantial evidence at best.

"Any chance you still have that laptop anywhere nearby?" Griff asked.

"Should be in a backpack behind my passenger seat. You're welcome to search my vehicle for it and take a look at anything you need to on the laptop."

"Excuse me for just a minute." Griff already had his cell phone to his ear as he stepped into the hallway. No doubt, he was delivering the message to one of his deputies.

A nurse scurried into the room. She gave a quick glance to each of the brothers before her gaze zeroed in on Chloe. "How are you feeling?"

"Better."

"My name is Wynonna. I'll be your nurse this evening. Is there anything I can get you to make you more comfortable?" Wynonna went over to the monitor and tapped a couple of buttons.

"Another blanket would be amazing." Chloe's skin had goose bumps. Aiden should've noticed that already.

The nurse nodded and made quick work of going to a cupboard and pulling out a fresh blanket that she immediately spread out on the bed. She picked up a big water container and checked it. "This is a little low." She scurried over to the sink and refilled it. "Your IV will take care of most of your hydration. Just in case you feel thirsty, you should have plenty of water." She set it down on the side table before repositioning for easy access. Then, she motioned toward a remote attached to the arm guard on the opposite side of the bed. "Press that button if you need help going to the restroom. With the amount of fluid intake you have going on it probably won't be too much longer. Don't be afraid to holler if you need anything else."

Chloe thanked her.

Wynonna smile before walking over to a whiteboard and writing her name. "Just in case you don't remember."

CHLOE WISHED she could remember something from the accident. At this point, that was the best she could classify what had happened even though from what she was being told there was nothing accidental about it. It was strange how the brain worked. She could remember plenty leading up to that event. Her mind was crystal clear now. Brain trauma could be a very interesting thing. And by interesting, she meant frustrating.

Griff came back into the room. "Deputy Sayer found your laptop. He's giving it to our tech guy, Arturo, so he can dig around and see what he can find. The blood splatter is under analysis and we don't have any hits on fingerprints yet."

She said a silent prayer for any break in the case. His expert had already been hacking away at her brother's laptop for days with nothing to show for it. The only passwords Chloe had were for her brother's bank account. She'd given those over freely, too.

"When I put out a call for help to search the area for you, your cousin Jefferson Collier showed up. He seemed concerned to the point of disruptive. Were the two of you very close?"

Really? "Never. No. Jefferson and I never really saw eye to eye. He was never a good influence on my brother growing up. Whenever the two of them got together, someone always ended up in trouble and that someone always seemed to be my brother, which was strange for a kid who normally made good grades in school and rarely talked back to our parents when they were alive."

Griff jotted down a few notes.

"I'm surprised he bothered to show up at all, actually. I've never made it a huge secret how I felt about him to him or my aunt. In fact, I stood up for my brother more than once and tried to point out the fact that Nicholas never got in trouble when Jefferson wasn't around. My parents discouraged them from hanging out and that usually worked."

"Would he have any reason, in your opinion, to harm your brother or you?"

Chloe thought about it for a long moment. "He always seemed to like Nicholas even though there was never any love lost between me and Jefferson." She wasn't aware that Nicholas was spending time with their cousin again. She could only imagine how Jefferson would've tried to use her baby brother. But Nicholas hadn't been showing any classic signs that he was headed down the wrong path. In fact, the news on the Nicholas front had been positive. He'd been returning her texts and calling to check on her instead of the other way around. He'd taken an interest in her work and started asking questions about her life.

"If Nicholas was spending time with Jefferson again there's a good chance he would have hid that from me."

"That's understandable. Based on what you said your brother might not want to upset you."

"He would've seen it as trying to protect me. So, you might find some interaction or contact between the two of them that I don't know about. Knowing Jefferson, though, he would somehow keep his involvement with my brother under the radar. I can see my cousin dropping by instead of calling or texting. Nicholas could've told him in advance when I visit. I've been consistent. I drive to see him on Wednesdays and Sundays. Wednesdays, I head to our folk's place after work to see him. Sundays, I drive down in the morning and try to spend as much of the day with him as I can. But I already told you that, didn't I?"

Griff was nodding his head. "It never hurts to go over information a second time. You'd be surprised how many times a little detail will come to light."

Chloe appreciated that Griff seemed to be trying to make her feel better about the memory slip. The doctor had mentioned it was common to have these kinds of blips and that hopefully everything would come back to her in a few days. He also warned, however, that sometimes the brain blocked out traumatic events and the details of tonight's crash may be tucked away forever.

The only reason she was frustrated about that was because she might've remembered something that could help the investigation. After her initial discussions with Griff over her brother's missing case, she realized how important time was when it came to investigations. The more time passed, the colder the trail.

Griff closed his notebook and tucked it into his shirt pocket. "Call me if you think of anything else even if it doesn't seem relevant. I'm available anytime and you already have my number."

"I will." Chloe appreciated the fact that Griff hadn't treated her like she was crazy when she insisted that her brother was missing, even though he'd written a suicide note and then disappeared. Griff had listened with empathy and without judgment. In fact, she was pretty certain any other officer would've written her response off as a reluctance to face the facts. It probably helped that she'd grown up in Gunner. And even though she loved her life in Austin, there was something about being home that stirred up feelings she'd been trying to ignore.

"I'll drop by tomorrow. Hopefully you'll be able to get at least some rest tonight." Griff gave Aiden a hug.

The thought of being stuck in a hospital overnight while her brother was out there somewhere possibly needing her was a hot poker in the chest. "Thank you for everything you're doing for me and my brother, Griff. I don't know if I expressed that well enough before."

Griff nodded and then left. As he was walking out the door, Aiden reclaimed his spot on the bed and took her hand in his.

Noah and Eli each took a chair. Were they planning to stick around?

"You guys don't have to be here. I mean, I appreciate the gesture but you guys have families and places to be." She may have said those words to all three of them except that she hoped in her heart that Aiden would stick around.

"We're here for as long as you need us." She remembered Noah from school. He was one of Aiden's older brothers. The Quinns took time to get to know. Once someone made it into their inner circle, though, he or she was in for life.

The dark thought struck that she might actually need security now. It was strange to think that someone might have an agenda that could end up with her missing or dead. But Eli had two little kids at home, and Noah had a new wife. Chloe had no idea what Aiden's relationship status was. A quick glance at his left hand provided way more relief than it should, considering the two of them had only ever been friends.

"I think I'll be okay. I mean, it's the hospital. There are nurses and doctors here, and security if the need arises." Although, she could scarcely wrap her brain around the fact that she might need it. Chloe, the person who never once even finagled on her taxes or cheated on her timesheet at the lab, was under attack. Her record was clean. Boring? Maybe. But her excitement in life had never come from taking from someone else or cheating a system. She'd always gone by the letter of the law.

The brothers glanced at each other and it was almost as if she could read their minds. They were thinking the same thing that she was. The need for security might just come up. Eli and Noah exchanged looks.

Noah spoke first to his older brother. "You have kids at home who will be up at the crack of dawn. Not to mention the fact that," he checked his watch, "duty on the ranch is gonna call faster than any of us would like. I'll take the first shift. Tell Dakota and the guys to work out covering my section. All I had on my plate tomorrow was running fences anyway."

Chloe knew from being Aiden's best friend in high school that fences had to be checked often to ensure their integrity. Loss of herds happened if a section of fence broke down that no one knew about; it was a basic duty on a cattle ranch. She'd always admired the fact that while most ranch owners checked fences using ATVs, Aiden and his brothers still rode horses. She'd asked Aiden about it once and he said that it made them feel more connected to the land and to the history of ranching. Being a Renaissance man was one of the things that she'd always liked about Aiden.

Eli started to put up a protest, but Noah's hands were already in the air waving at him.

"I insist. Now go home and get some rest. One of us is gonna need to cover at the ranch."

This time, Eli nodded. Aiden let go of Chloe's hand and she immediately felt the cold air where his warmth had been. He stood and hugged his brother, thanking him for coming so quickly and on such short notice.

Eli acted like it was nothing. Chloe knew different. As close as she was to her baby brother, they'd never quite had the close bond the Quinn boys did. And as men, clearly still did. A part of her heart yearned to have that kind of family life around her. It had been a really long time since she and Nicholas had lost their parents.

A surprising amount of emotion filled her, causing water to well in her eyes. In general, she never took a step back and looked at family life. In fact, she'd almost cut herself off from any possibility of marriage and children. Nicholas had been her worry since he left for the military and especially since he returned.

That same voice inside her head returned, reminding her that her younger brother was strong despite what had happened to him.

7

"It's good to see you again, Aiden."

Those words from Chloe were an unexpected shot to Aiden's heart. "Same here."

Almost half an hour had passed and Noah had curled up on the chair in the room. His eyes were closed and his even breathing said he was taking a nap. Were it not for him in the room, Chloe's words would've made them feel like the only two people in the world.

"Do you think you can get any rest?" Chloe looked tired. Even so, she'd still be the prettiest woman in any room hands down.

"Every time I think about closing my eyes, I panic a little bit. I probably shouldn't admit that I'm scared. It probably doesn't make me sound as strong as I am. There it is."

"Being afraid doesn't make you weak. Fear keeps people alive. The only time it's a problem is when it stops us from doing the things most important to us. If fear keeps you from jumping out of a plane without a parachute, I would never consider that a bad thing." He spoke with a smile and when she returned it more of that lightning struck his chest again.

"I can't believe I didn't think about this before now but what happened to my purse and my cell phone?"

"As far as I know, Griff has them in evidence." He noticed how quickly she'd changed the subject about her fears and wished there was something more he could do to ease them.

"What does that mean?"

"I'm sure he'll bring them with him tomorrow. He'll probably need to have them dusted for prints just in case. This attempt to..." He didn't know how to fill in the blank. An attempt to kidnap her? An attempt to silence her permanently? Aiden had no idea what the person or persons' intentions were.

"I just keep thinking maybe my brother will call and tell me this is all some kind of prank and that he's totally fine. It's all so surreal. You know?" Chloe could always take care of herself. She'd always been thick-skinned and able to stand up to bullies. And she had this unique ability to somehow, sometimes still be incredibly vulnerable. Aiden ignored more of those jolts to his traitorous heart. Yes, she was still beautiful. Even more so now. And he couldn't forget her intelligence, especially when he was pretty certain that same sharp sense of humor still worked behind those worried eyes. She cared. A lot. Chloe could take or leave most people but when she went in with someone, she went all in.

"I'm not sure if you're up to speed on some of the stuff that's been going on around town and affecting my family. Now, I can see how screwed up that must've been for them. And now I feel a hell of a lot guiltier about not being here to support them. I can only imagine what must be running through your mind about your brother."

She nodded. Their gazes locked and held for a moment longer than was probably a good idea. He resisted the urge to lean forward and press a kiss to that tiny mole just above her upper lip. He'd always been fascinated by that damn mole. Even now, he wondered how it would feel against his own lips.

Since this wasn't the time for those thoughts, he shelved them. He'd become a master at compartmentalizing. Moving on.

"You must have some theories about what might've happened to your brother. You want to bounce them off me?" He needed to refocus back onto the case.

"I hadn't really thought too much about Jefferson, to be honest. Now that Griff has brought him up, I can't help but wonder if he and my brother were talking again. And I have no idea what Jefferson is into now. I tried to mind my own business when we were younger. Now that I live in Austin, it's been really easy to avoid him."

"What about your aunt? Would it do any good to talk to her?"

"She passed away about five years ago."

"I'm sorry." In five years, a person could blow through an inheritance.

"She and I weren't really close, and she believed that her son walked on water when he didn't, so we didn't see eye to eye. She seemed to start having an even bigger problem with me after my parents' accident. She said I didn't handle their funerals correctly, and she wanted to be in charge of the estate. She tried to force me to sell their home and land, so we stopped talking to each other."

"Do you mind if I ask why you held onto the house and property if you lived in Austin and Nicholas was away?"

"I kept it for my brother to have a place to come home to when he had leave from the military; I also think I kind of always hoped if he had a place here that he would maybe move back. He's so young and he's been through so much...I just wanted him to have something stable in his life. You know?" The shakiness in her voice said she was trying not to get emotional.

Aiden squeezed her hand tighter for support. He did understand. "Nicholas might be younger than you but that doesn't make him young, if you know what I mean. He was old enough to serve his country and serve it well. That doesn't sound like a little kid to me." Aiden could see that Chloe, like always, still looked out for everyone else before herself. Aiden couldn't help but wonder who had her back?

More of that familiar guilt struck, this time for ditching town and leaving her behind to deal with everything life had handed her. The guilt was racking up.

"He was a good soldier. People should know that about him." The defeat in her voice was another wake-up call.

"Nicholas may have gotten on the wrong side of trouble every once in a while, but he was a good person. Good athlete, too. Coach used to talk about him to us upperclassman all the time."

"You never told me that."

Aiden smirked. "I couldn't have you going back home and telling your brother all these great things coach was saying about him. His head would get so big he wouldn't be able to fit it through the locker room door."

Chloe laughed. Her free hand went to her forehead, like laughing caused her a little too much pain. This time, when their eyes met he saw little bit of that spark coming back. Good. She needed to remember how strong she truly was.

A GOOD LAUGH HURT.

But it felt good to hear good things about Nicholas again. For months all she'd felt was sorrow for him, and before that, it seemed like all she did was worry. "Do you remember that time he caught me sneaking out my window to meet you?"

"You mean that time we ended up skinny-dipping in old man Chester's Pond?"

"I had on a sports bra and short shorts. There was no 'we' about it."

Making Aiden laugh put a smile on Chloe's face. In that moment, they were still fifteen-year-olds without a care in the world. She'd seen that same look in Aiden's eyes countless times; it always faded right before he'd declare it was time to go home and yet he would never talk about what made home so bad with her. Back then, she'd always seen him as the strong silent type. Sure, he would open up a little bit at times when they were alone. Usually, he was making a joke or being silly. Those genuine laughs of his were like pure gold.

His smile always faded too fast.

"What about that other time you convinced my dad to let me

borrow his car?" She still couldn't believe her dad had handed over the keys that night.

"What are you talking about? It was a matter of life and death. Of course, he had to hand over the keys."

She tilted her head to the side and shot him that look. The one that called him on his BS. "You had me believing there was some kind of emergency and then where did we end up?"

"Drive-in movie theater. And for the record it was an emergency. I didn't have my truck and you can't walk into a drive-in movie theater. Besides, it was probably the only one left in the state of Texas."

"They used to play all those crazy older movies. I can't even remember one. Everyone always just walked around and goofed off." She didn't want to mention the fact that Aiden usually ended up meeting up with his girlfriend or finding a new one at the drive-in. Her best friend had been quite the playboy back then. And she couldn't exactly blame high school girls for practically falling at his feet, he'd been one of the hottest guys in school. Forget the fact when they met up with any of his brothers or cousins, which reminded her. "Remember all those times when people made that joke about you, your brothers and cousins?"

The look on his face said he did. "Oh, no. Not you, too. I thought that old joke would eventually burn out."

"I said it then and I'll say it now...if you guys ever wanted to raise serious money for charity, the way to do it would be a Quinn calendar. It'd be hotter than any of those half-naked firemen ones."

"Hold on a second. Did you just call me hot?"

"No." Her response came quickly. A little too quickly. This seemed like a good time to be grateful for the fact that the lights were dimmed because she was pretty sure a red blush had just crawled up her neck and flamed her cheekbones. She could feel the rash forming, and suddenly the temperature felt like a hundred degrees in the room. Thankfully, Noah picked that moment to adjust his position on her bed.

By the time he shifted his gaze back to her, the flame was on a low simmer. She could conceal that.

"Anyway," he continued, "if memory serves, we talked your brother out of busting you by taking him on a fishing and camping trip with me and my brothers. He caught the biggest catfish out of all of us. His smile was ear-to-ear."

"I'm pretty sure he thought he was the coolest kid in Texas for getting to hang out with older boys and the most popular boys in school."

"We weren't—"

"Don't even try to deny it, Aiden Matthew Quinn."

"I haven't been called by my full name since the last time I pushed Marianne to the brink of her patience. I think I swiped a couple of her cookies on Christmas Eve morning without realizing those weren't meant for us. She'd promised them for a cookie exchange and had to bring a certain number." A low rumble sounded from deep in his chest when he broke into a laugh this time. "She couldn't show up with ten cookies instead of twelve. You know Marianne. If she gives someone her word it can be counted on."

"One of her many wonderful qualities. She was a saint to bring up the seven of you and look at how you guys turned out. You're all good people."

He cocked a dark brow. "My brothers are. I'm not so sure about me."

"You were. You *are*." She realized they'd been talking for a solid hour. He must be worn out after a long drive, searching for her and now sitting in the hospital. She scooted over and patted the spot beside her. "Did you make that fifteen-hour drive straight through?"

"I sure did."

"Then lay down here with me." It dawned on her that there might be some woman out there who would be greatly offended by the fact that a man she was in a relationship might be in bed with someone from his past. A hospital bed, but still.

Although, to be fair, Chloe and Aiden's relationship had always been platonic, which is why it didn't bother her that Noah was still asleep in the chair. It had always been based on friendship. And even though she'd been attracted to him, there was no way she was having her heart trampled on by the best-looking guy in class. And since she didn't want to offend a person she hadn't even met yet, she asked, "Are you seeing anyone? I mean, I'm not asking you to go out. I'm just trying to make sure no one can walk through that door and get the wrong idea."

Aiden's back was to her as she finished her sentence, so she couldn't get a good read on his reaction. Until he took the spot beside her and leaned back. His face was a show of perfectly straight, perfectly white teeth.

"You can wipe that smirk off your face, buddy. I'm trying to be considerate."

"If I was in a relationship, and that's a big *if*, you'd be the first to know."

Chloe had no idea what that meant and had no plans to ask tonight. Instead, she relaxed beside him, side-by-side on her bed, like they'd done so many times when they were younger.

She must've fallen asleep because the next thing she knew her eyes opened. The low hum of two male voices caught her attention. She blinked blurry eyes and quickly scanned the room. The space beside her was empty and Aiden was huddled up with two of his brothers, Noah and one of the twins. She could never distinguish between Isaac and Liam.

A quick glance at the clock on the wall said she'd been asleep for an hour. She had no idea how it was possible, but her head hurt even worse. The dull throb was almost worse than the sharp pain it had replaced. For a second, she thought about buzzing the nurse to ask for pain medication. The ache wasn't bad enough for that and her doctor said it was best if she could hold off until she was in the clear for a concussion.

Satisfied that she was in good hands with the Quinn brothers, she closed her eyes again and half-listened in case there was any information about Nicholas that she needed to be aware of. She must've dozed off again because the next time she opened her eyes Aiden sat beside her, sipping from one of those paper cups. Coffee smelled and sounded amazing about now.

One of the twins had replaced Noah, who she assumed had gone home. Chloe couldn't help but marvel at how tight-knit the Quinn brothers' relationships seemed, especially since so many of them had been gone from Gunner for so long. Her family had been close when her parents were alive. Missing them was still a physical ache when she focused on her loss.

Even though she worked long hours at the lab and volunteered for every extra shift she could, holidays and weekends included, she couldn't keep herself busy enough not to miss her family. Her mom had worked the pre-kindergarten class at a preschool and her father had been a middle school history teacher. They didn't have a lot of money growing up, not that Chloe had ever really noticed. They'd had food and clothes. Her mother had owned a sewing machine and their favorite place had been the thrift shop. She'd fix up their finds. Her brother, Nicholas, had been shy and athletic. She didn't get the sports gene, strictly a late-nights at the library, study hard kind of girl.

Looking back, half the attraction of being close friends with Aiden Quinn had probably been because of how dangerous he seemed to her. They'd been opposites in every sense of the word. Whereas Aiden wasn't close to his father, she and her parents had a good relationship. She always looked out for her younger brother and since both of her parents worked, babysitting fell to her most of the time. She didn't mind. Nicholas had always been a good kid when he was around the right influence.

Aiden's hand covered hers, stirring a feeling of warmth low in her belly that quickly spread throughout her body. Her hand twitched and she opened her eyes to find him studying her.

"I was wondering if you were starting to wake up." His low timbre traveled all over her, following the warm feeling she'd had moments before.

The thought she could get used to waking up like this almost made her laugh out loud. "Any chance I can get a sip of coffee?"

"I can do better than that. I can get you a whole cup." Aiden started to get up anyway but the sudden knock at the door had him shooting to his feet in a heartbeat.

The head that timidly peeked in belonged to Kingston Herbert. She recognized Nicholas's sponsor immediately.

"Come in, Kingston." Chloe nodded at Aiden, who looked to her for clarification.

Kingston had a lot in common with Nicholas. Both had played sports in high school. Nicholas had played football, whereas Kingston's game of choice had been basketball. Both had been top athletes for their schools and were similar in age. They'd signed up to serve at eighteen, albeit in different branches of the military; their similarities were probably the reasons they'd been matched up in the first place.

"I heard you were in here, and I hope it's okay that I decided to come check on you." Kingston's eyes flashed toward Aiden, who set his cup of coffee down. He stood in an athletic stance, feet apart and arms folded across a broad chest, and to someone who didn't know him she figured his posture could be threatening. Tension was so thick, it felt like a fog filled the room. Rather than get upset about it, Chloe appreciated Aiden's defensiveness.

"Kingston, I'd like you to meet an old friend of mine. Meet Aiden Quinn. Aiden, this is Kingston Herbert. He was...*is*...my brother's counselor." Aiden didn't soften his stance when he extended his hand toward Kingston.

"The pleasure is all mine." Kingston's accent suddenly became thick as he stepped into the handshake, and he looked a little surprised at the firm grip he got in return. Even though he was originally from a small town in Louisiana, there was hardly anything left of what he'd said had been a strong Cajun accent at one time until now.

8

"Why don't you take my cup?"

Aiden picked up his coffee cup from the side table where he'd stashed it when Kingston entered the room and then handed it to Chloe. Liam stood; he sized Kingston up and must've decided the guy was no match for Aiden.

"I don't mind making a coffee run. I can use a fresh cup myself." He looked to Chloe. "How do you take yours?"

"Usually? With lots of cream and sugar. Today? Strong and black would fit the bill perfectly." She pushed to sitting using the remote control on the side of her bed. With the press of a button the bed started molding to her new position. "Thank you..." Her gaze narrowed and it dawned on Aiden that she couldn't tell which twin she was talking to.

"Liam," Aiden whispered out of the side of his mouth with a wink. The smile he received in return was worth the lack of sleep he'd had in the past twenty-four hours. It was also stronger than the jolt of caffeine he'd had after downing his first cup a few minutes ago.

"Is there any news about Nicholas?" Kingston stayed at the doorway until Chloe waved him in. The man stepped lightly around Aiden, as he should. He had on a long sleeve shirt and jeans. His baseball cap was on backwards and his long hair was pulled back in a ponytail.

"No. Nothing so far."

"I thought I heard you were going back to Austin."

"Right. My brother's dog turned up, so I turned around."

"Ah. I understand." Aiden noted that Kingston didn't ask how Zeus was doing. Wouldn't he care about Nicholas's dog?

"Would you like to sit down?" Chloe was probably just being polite, so it shouldn't be fingernails on a chalkboard that she'd invited Kingston to stick around. Or maybe it was just the fact that he seemed to know more about her and her life than Aiden did. He recognized that for the out of the blue feeling it was.

"Sure. I can only stay a couple of minutes, though." Kingston sat on the edge of the seat that Liam had occupied a few moments ago. He scooted it closer toward the bed, which was on the opposite side of where Aiden stood.

Chloe seemed to trust Kingston but Aiden didn't like him. He seemed shifty with his two-day-old stubble on his chin. Aiden didn't like the way Kingston seemed unable to look either one of them in the eyes for long.

"What has you in Gunner?" Chloe asked.

"I was, uh, just here to check on another one of the people I sponsor last night."

"Oh, really?" Chloe's brow shot up and Aiden made a mental note to ask her about it later.

"Yes." Kingston's gaze dropped down and to the left, usually a sign someone was lying or covering. "I was meeting with someone at a coffee shop near the highway when I heard there'd been an accident involving Nicholas's sister. When I asked about it, the coffee shop owner said he heard it was pretty bad. I came out to help but must've gotten there too late, and everyone was gone. I asked around and found out you were okay and in the hospital. I decided to check on you before I left town today."

Aiden guessed news traveled fast in a small town. Information about the search party would most likely get out, considering all the deputies had been called in along with quite a few volunteer firefighters, who'd shown on the scene. His family name made news, too. His involvement would only put more of a spotlight on Chloe. Living in Colorado, he'd distanced himself from the Quinn family name and had been living a quiet life. It was strange to suddenly be the center of attention again.

"I know my brother thought you were a good sponsor. Thank you for everything you were trying to do for him."

"I only wish I could've made a bigger impact." Kingston clasped his hands together. "There must've been something I could've done to stop him..."

The counselor dropped his head low. It was probably the fact that Aiden had grown up with an uncle for a sheriff that made him suspicious of everyone, of Kingston. The guy was either putting on a very good act or he was deeply bothered. Aiden understood that as a sponsor, Kingston would care about someone he was helping. This seemed dramatic...and something else. Forced? Besides, Nicholas was a missing person. In theory, he could walk through that door at any minute.

"We'll find him, Kingston. My brother has to be out there somewhere. Knowing Nicholas, he just got lost on a camping trip and Zeus found his way home first." Even Aiden realized it was impossible to have a death without a body. The note was puzzling, but the timing of Chloe's so-called accident last night confirmed at least in his mind that foul play was involved. She was convinced her brother hadn't written the note despite admitting it had been penned in his handwriting. In Aiden's book, that meant Nicholas had been forced.

Liam returned with two coffees in hand and Aiden thought Kingston's head might actually hit the ceiling for how high he jumped. He sidestepped the chair and ended up leaning against the windowsill. He almost couldn't get out of Liam's way fast enough.

Maybe Aiden needed to dial down his aggressive attitude toward Kingston. The man was obviously on edge and Aiden wasn't making it any easier for him. No doubt, Griff would've already spoken to Nicholas's sponsor, especially since he seemed to be someone of importance to Nicholas. He made another mental note to circle back to Griff and get his impression of Kingston as Liam handed a fresh cup of coffee to Chloe.

"Is it true there had to be a search party called out to find you last night?" Kingston asked Chloe.

"I must've banged my head on something, left my SUV, and wandered into the woods. Zeus may have run off and I might've chased after him. I have no idea what happened, but I seem to be okay now. In fact, I'm sure my doctor will be in pretty soon. If all goes well, I might be able to leave this place." Chloe smiled warmly at Kingston, and a knot tightened in Aiden's gut.

He returned the gesture and more of those fingernails-on-a-chalkboard sounded in Aiden's mind. Liam reclaimed his seat and sipped his own coffee. He had his phone out and he seemed to be studying the screen. He sent a text and Aiden assumed his brother was checking in at the ranch until his own cell phone buzzed.

Aiden fished it out of his pocket and glanced at the screen. The text was from Liam, who sat across the room. *I don't like this guy.*

It looked like Aiden and Liam were on the same page. But that didn't mean Kingston was guilty. Griff mentioned that he'd be stopping by the hospital today, though Aiden wanted to get Chloe out of here because if Kingston knew where she was that meant other people did, too. Call him paranoid but he didn't appreciate word of her whereabouts getting around town and especially not after what happened last night. If someone had done something to Nicholas and that same person was now targeting Chloe, her life could be in danger.

Then again, she'd been in an accident. If someone wanted her dead wouldn't they have finished the job last night?

"I'd better head out." Kingston seemed eager not to overstay his welcome. But then, his big eyes when he'd first walked into the room might have indicated that he wasn't expecting anyone other than Chloe to be here.

Aiden typed one word in response to Liam's text. *Same.*

"Thanks for stopping by to check on me, Kingston. I'm fine, or at least I will be."

Chloe figured she wouldn't be truly okay until she found her brother safe. In fact, she was eager to get out of this hospital and onto the search for Nicholas. Now that she had help from Aiden, it occurred to her that she might actually get some traction on her brother's case. At the very least, she could get the inside track on the investigation.

The minute Kingston walked out the door she caught the look exchanged between Aiden and his brother.

"What's that about?" she asked Aiden before taking a sip of her fresh brew Liam had given her. The coffee was bad enough for her to make a face but she took another sip anyway needing the caffeine.

"You want my honest opinion?"

"Give it to me straight, Aiden. When have I ever wanted you to lie to me?" She couldn't be more serious.

"Fair enough. Personally, I don't like the guy." He held his hand up, palm out. "Don't ask me why specifically. It's just my impression of him. He seemed a little bit too nervous when he saw Liam and me. And why at the end of May when it's friggin ninety degrees outside with high humidity would he be wearing long sleeves?"

"That's not exactly a reason not to like someone, is it?"

Liam nodded. Apparently, neither one appreciated the way Kingston dressed. Typical ranchers, who were known for sticking to a stable of jeans and T-shirts. Chloe didn't want to notice how well the cotton on Aiden's pressed against his chest when he moved, outlining muscles for days.

"Plus, how much do you really know about the guy?" Aiden reclaimed his seat next to her.

"Not a lot. My brother thought he was a decent guy. Admittedly, Nicholas had sort of turned inside himself after what had happened to him overseas. After Kingston started visiting, I saw a few positive changes in my brother."

"I'm not suggesting there was a problem in the beginning. What do you really know about Kingston Herbert?" Aiden had a point.

She shrugged in response. "I really don't know much about him other than the fact that he's been an addict, too."

"Which is all well and good as long as no one relapses or gets themselves in some kind of trouble. It sounds like we don't really know what Kingston was really about before he signed up to be a sponsor in the first place. Do you know how long he's been in the program?"

After Aiden's questions, she realized how little she knew about the guy. "I don't know much more than the basics."

A knock at the door interrupted their conversation. As she'd hoped, it was Dr. Hill. He came in and checked her chart.

"How are you doing this morning?" he asked after shaking hands with Liam and Aiden.

"I still have a whopper of a dull headache right between my eyes. The back of my head feels like it was split open yesterday. Other than that, a few aches and pains. Nothing that a warm bath couldn't fix."

Dr. Hill smiled. "After what you went through, that's not bad. Can you tell me what day it is?"

"Since yesterday was Wednesday, that makes today Thursday."

Dr. Hill nodded. He went through the same questions as he had last night, asking who the president was and then her own name and where she lived. He asked for her home address. All of which she answered correctly.

When he smiled and scribbled a couple of notes on her chart before closing it and looking up at her she knew she was going to get the news she'd been hoping for. "Everything looks good. You're cleared to go home. I'd prefer you took a break from doing any physical work. My orders are to take it easy for a couple of days and if you have any nausea or vomiting come back to see me immediately."

"Will do, Doctor." She was almost giddy at the idea of getting out of the hospital. A shower, a toothbrush and her own PJs sounded like heaven right now. But those were in Austin and she was planning to stick around Gunner for a few days until she could drive again.

Aiden thanked Dr. Hill for everything he'd done for her before the doctor made his exit.

Liam stood and stretched out his arms. He looked at his brother when he said, "I'll take a slow walk downstairs to get your truck. Eli gave me the keys last night. Where do you want me to drive you guys?"

"I was thinking of coming home to the ranch. Think anyone would mind if Chloe stayed with us for a few days?"

"Are you kidding me? Marianne would be in heaven. She already is and she keeps saying how there are still empty rooms in Casa Grande that need filling." Liam laughed and so did Aiden.

"Well then we'll meet you downstairs as soon as I can bust her out of here." The brothers hugged, and their show of affection caused a surprising tear to spring to Chloe's eye. She tucked her chin to her chest and forced a cough.

Liam disappeared down the hall and she was pretty sure Aiden gave him some kind of instructions before he left.

"Let me just fire off a text to Griff and let him know where we're headed and then I can help you get dressed or whatever you need." Aiden took his phone out of his pocket and sent a text. He looked up and locked eyes with Chloe. "Do you have any idea where they put your clothes last night?"

"Yes. In that cupboard right over there." She pointed. "But I'm sure it'll take like two more hours before I can get out of here because somebody from billing will have to come up and I'll have to sign my life away."

Aiden's back was to her, so when he spoke she wasn't sure she heard him right.

"Say that again."

"You don't have to worry about getting a bill. You're free to leave whenever you want to walk out that door."

The look on her face must've been pretty dumbfounded because when he turned with her folded clothes in his hands, he stopped to explain. "T.J. donated an entire wing in this hospital years ago after our mother passed away. Liam is stopping by the billing office to let them know not to send a bill to you."

"That's not a good idea, Aiden. I don't want to be indebted to anyone—"

"It's not like that. You wouldn't be—"

She folded her arms across her chest. "I have insurance, Aiden. I have some savings. I can pay my own bill."

It wasn't like she had a reason to spend her money. She'd been saving for a new car but that could wait. Hers still worked fine. Or at least it had. Now, she'd have to wait for the front end to be repaired.

"My father set up some kind of fund. The whole point of it is to take care of bills for people. So, technically, *I'm* not doing anything. My father is." She was pretty certain that Aiden had just told her a little white lie. She decided this one time to let him get away with it, but she was pretty certain he had no idea what his father did on a day-to-day basis and had made a point of not figuring it out for years.

"Just promise me we'll figure something out so I can pay your family back, Aiden."

His grin was ear to ear when he said, "I'm sure we can work out an *arrangement.*"

Chloe turned away from him, praying he couldn't see the red blush as it crawled up her cheeks or the way her pulse began to pound at the base of her neck. Her stomach gave a little traitorous flip, that freefall sensation like she'd just jumped out of an airplane without wearing a parachute returned.

"Just hand over my clothes and quit kidding around." By the time she lifted her face she'd gotten a hold of her physical reaction to him. But she turned just in time to see his eyes darken with something that looked a lot like attraction, causing a sensual shiver to skitter across her skin.

"Let me know if you need help putting those on." The smirk on his face said that was meant to be a joke. His voice, however, dropped a few octaves and came out husky.

Chloe avoided contact when she took the folded-up outfit she'd had on yesterday. Yesterday felt like it had happened days ago. In fact, the last three, correction, now four days felt like a lifetime.

Trying to stand on her own caused her to feel a little lightheaded. She struggled with a bout of nausea, as well. But after a few tentative steps toward the bathroom she started to regain her footing.

One glance in the mirror and she was suddenly horrified to realize her hair didn't look like it had seen a brush this month. It was odd to think that suddenly she wished she had a little foundation and lipstick on her. She was pretty certain Aiden had seen her looking much worse. Especially the time he knocked on her window in eleventh grade when she had the flu. He'd insisted that she open up and let him come inside. When her father had come to check on her and the two of them had almost been busted, he spent a solid fifteen minutes in the pitch-black closet while her mother made a big deal out of the fever that had spiked.

And yet, Aiden had been undaunted. He'd somehow managed to spend half the night with her, comforting her while still making it home in time for roll call in the barn at four a.m.

Chloe's muscles were tight, and her limbs had never felt stiffer. Every step caused pain, and every movement made her want to freeze. She needed to push through it, like always.

Suddenly, that didn't feel like enough.

It might be the feeling of facing her own mortality that caused her to want so much more than to just push through life. Because all too soon birthdays would come until they stacked together and eventually caused her hair to turn gray. What would she look back on? What would she truly have to be proud of?

Pushing through life?

9

C hloe quickly dressed, as quickly as she could under the circumstances, and stepped into her hospital room. Aiden stood staring out the window. She glanced at the clock and it was half past ten in the morning.

"Ready?" he asked.

"I don't think I've ever been more ready for anything in my life than to leave this place." He walked toward her and then offered an arm to steady her. She took it.

"I'm pretty sure it's customary to be wheeled out of here in a wheelchair. How much of a rebel do you feel like today?" That twinkle in his eye was back. He was all mischief and danger. And comfort? Although none of those words made sense in the same sentence, usually, this was Aiden. He was all of that and more for Chloe.

"James Dean doesn't have anything on me."

"Since the doctor cleared you for takeoff, I say we get out of here." He had that devilish grin that had caused a line of teenage girls to form outside the door to the locker room at school after a game, waiting and hoping to get a date.

Since she and Aiden had always been best friends, Chloe had lost count of the number of times someone in her friendship circle tried to get her to set them up with Aiden. Even then, her heart broke a little bit with every request. She'd had a huge crush on him even then and had been too scared to do anything about it.

"Let's do this." This time, she matched his smile, wattage for wattage, when she beamed at him. For a split second she thought she saw an emotion pass behind his eyes that she couldn't quite pinpoint. Suddenly, the fact that she could only be described as a hot mess didn't matter. It was probably just their history that brought on a yearning so deep she could've sworn it reached to the deepest places in her heart.

Rather than analyze it, she nudged him to get moving.

In the hallway, she was pretty certain she heard a nurse ask her to stop. But Aiden swiftly walked her to the elevator and then turned and pushed the button to close the doors before anyone could reach them. It was odd because it was as free as she felt in longer than she could remember, and she was most definitely not a rule breaker.

She chalked her emotions up to being with Aiden again. He'd always had the ability to make her forget anything that had been upsetting to her, a bad test grade or being late to class and getting yelled at once again by Mrs. Bade, the crankiest homeroom teacher in all of Chloe's primary school educational career. She and Aiden had joked countless times that the woman must wake up and kick puppies before yelling at innocent babies to make them cry as she passed by.

No one was safe around Bad Bade. God, it felt good to remember simpler times before she'd lost her parents, and her brother had become almost unrecognizable. Speaking of Nicholas, she needed to come up with a plan to restart her search. The flyers she'd printed out to hang at local businesses and bus stops were still in the back of her SUV.

Liam was already waiting with the truck. He relinquished the driver seat and climbed in the back as she moved to the passenger side. Aiden took the wheel. He and his brother talked a little bit about basic ranch business on the way. Their conversation was a reassuring hum in her ear as she stared out the window and watched as the houses thinned and the trees thickened.

A shiver raced up her spine as he neared the area of last night's car crash. "This is the spot, isn't it?"

"Yes. It is." She appreciated that Aiden didn't see the need to continue talking or tell her that it was all going to be okay. Nothing would be all right again until her brother was home safe where he belonged.

Chloe studied the wooded area, hoping and praying that she would remember something that could be helpful to Griff's investigation. When nothing came, she sank back in her seat. She scanned the area, wondering if her brother was still in Gunner or if he'd been kidnapped and taken somewhere else. He could be anywhere by now. The fact that Zeus had shown up had given her a renewed sense of hope. False hope?

The likelihood that Zeus would have been taken with her brother was slim to none. Zeus most likely had been let out of the yard. The gate had been left open. He may have witnessed Nicholas's kidnapping and tried to follow. Or Nicholas might've been on the run and Zeus tried to track him.

Turning onto the drive to Quinnland Ranch brought back a flood of memories. Aiden zipped past the security gate and it wasn't long before Casa Grande came into view. The house had always been big and beautiful, and it made her feel a little better to see that nothing had changed. She thanked Liam as Aiden parked, noting that he'd situated his truck as far from the house as he could.

"I'll let Marianne know the two of you are here. You both have to be starving by now." Liam tipped his hat and exited the vehicle.

It occurred to her that it must be awfully strange for Aiden to be back after all these years. He sat there, studying the main house and she wished she could read his thoughts.

"Remember that time when we were in the barn and Dakota got so mad at us because...what were we doing again?"

"Who knows? With us, anything goes." At least that comment got a smile out of him. She'd smiled more in the past twelve hours than she had in longer than she could remember, longer than she wanted to remember. "I saw a lab coat in your SUV. What do you do for a living?"

"I run a laboratory." The obvious answer caused them both to laugh and it broke the tension. "I'm actually kind of serious about that. I worked my way up from lab tech and now I run my own lab."

"Good that you're putting your biology degree to use." She couldn't agree more. Her parents had left a little life insurance policy that had covered school for her. Nicholas had used his money to buy a new Jeep and finish high school. The rest was going toward keeping the house where they grew up in the family.

"You never told me what you do for a living now, Aiden."

"I guess I haven't." He scratched his chin and she playfully tapped him on the arm. "Okay. Okay. I design and build barns for a living. I pretty much cover the whole Southwest and have built some magnificent structures." There was so much pride in his voice.

"What made you decide to go into that line of work?" Although, she could see it. He'd always been stronger in math than her. She'd loved biology, whereas he'd always sketched out buildings and figured out dimensions.

"I was pretty damn qualified to do it, if you ask me," he teased. "I mean, I did spend my childhood in a barn."

"Well, partially in a barn. The other part was spent out there." She nodded away from the house.

"As I recall, a good portion of my high school years were spent sneaking in your window."

A blush crawled up her neck, which was strange because there hadn't been anything sexual about their relationship back then. Sure, she'd had a crush on him that had grown into something she didn't want to admit to even now. "I was thinking about that time you almost got caught and ended up in my closet for what seemed like forever. I'm pretty certain you fell asleep and I heard you snoring."

"Right. You had the flu. I was worried about the fact that you didn't show up for school for like three days. I was bored out of my mind and had no one to talk to."

"Somehow, I doubt that's true."

"What?" He sounded offended with that one word.

"You had sports and pretty much any high school cheerleader you wanted."

He shook his head. And then he got really quiet.

Was it a sore subject?

"Why haven't you come home in so long, Aiden? What happened to make you stay away and not look back?" She'd been wanting to ask him that question for a decade or longer.

"T.J. happened. I remember that we got into this really bad argument. The details are fuzzy now, but it seemed like a big deal at the time. I mainly recall the intense anger I felt toward him. I had a lot of anger back then anyway, figured it was par for the course for a teenager. But that day, he pushed me over the edge. I had a hot temper anyway and he really seemed to know how to push my buttons."

Chloe couldn't imagine having a fight with her parents. Granted, their relationship was far from perfect. If they were angry, though, they actually sat down and talked things out. The house rule was that no one went to bed still mad. It worked most of the time. She could think of a few times in her teenage years when she faked not being upset just so she wouldn't have to sit at the kitchen table and hash out her feelings.

Looking back, it was probably the reason her family was so close. There was a lot of genuine love between them. The thought of what Aiden had gone through with his own father had always haunted her.

She risked asking the question he was never willing to answer. "So what happened?"

"I just remember the feeling of wishing that my mother was alive and he was the one who was dead. Kind of a jerk move, huh?" Her heart ached for his pain, for the fact that he'd held this in so long. Aiden had never mentioned anything about his mother when they were young. It was as though he'd locked the memory of her so far away that it had become untouchable.

"Not really. I mean, your father was supposed to be the more mature one between the two of you. You'd like to think that he could rise above an angry situation and not purposely pick a fight."

"Well, our family didn't work like that. We didn't talk about things. Anything. And especially not the pain that came with losing our mother. That subject was taboo. So, being the teenager that I was, I threw that in his face. I told him he was the reason our mother was dead because he treated her like some child-bearing factory. He was hurt by my comments. I'd heard a long time ago that he never quite got over the death of my mother. So I threw fuel onto that fire until he just blew up and said a few horrible things to me. Next thing I know, I have him pinned against the wall. My fist is reared back and I'm ready to take that punch."

"Why didn't you?"

"Because I hesitated long enough to realize how wrong that would be. That it wasn't the kind of person I wanted to be. Even then, I knew that I didn't want to be a jerk who threw a punch to solve a problem."

"You were never that guy, Aiden." She couldn't recall a time when she'd seen him angry at her. There'd never been a harsh word spoken between them in all the years they'd been friends.

"I failed miserably that day and all I could see was the disappointment that would have been in my mother's eyes. Then, I realized being around T.J. did that to me. *He* knew how to press that one button and hit that last nerve that would just cause me to be at the point of wanting to explode. I'd want to take my anger out on him. Reality smacked me like a punch. *She* wouldn't have wanted that. My mom. So, I feel like I failed her in the worst possible way. The feeling of shame wasn't something I could deal with. And since my father was the cause of it, I swore him off."

HEARING those words out loud made Aiden realize that in pushing his father away, he closed himself off to his entire family. Setting his feelings aside, burying them deep, had always been his strong suit. Until now. Being back in Gunner with his brothers, with Chloe forced him to see everything he'd been missing.

"I know you said you came back for your brothers, but aren't you the least bit curious about what your dad has to say?"

"Don't get me wrong, there's not really a lot of love lost between him and me. He is my father, though. I don't wish anything bad on him."

"You don't trust him, either." It was more question than statement.

"I think you know where I stand." Aiden realized he'd been gripping the steering wheel so tight his knuckles went white.

"I always thought something happened that made you turn your back on everything and everyone back home." The hurt in her voice was a stab to the heart.

"Is that what you thought I did to you?" Hearing it said like that, he couldn't deny its truth. Still, it bothered him that he'd hurt her feelings. Damn, there he went being focused on himself when he should've thought about how his actions might be hurting her. All Aiden could say was that he was glad he wasn't an eighteen-year-old anymore. A kid too intent on his own problems and not enough focus on the world around him. "I thought I did you a favor by leaving and not looking back."

Aiden couldn't exactly identify the sound that came out of her mouth. It was too strong to be a grunt.

"How so, Aiden? I lost my best friend." She didn't wait for him to respond. Instead she grabbed the door opener and shoved her shoulder into the door. Before he could say anything, she was standing outside of the truck, arms folded.

"Chloe, I'm sorry. I didn't mean—"

She waved him off before he could finish his sentence. When her eyes came up to meet his, they'd changed. He couldn't quite put into words what he saw except that he knew in his heart a wall had come up between them.

"It's nothing, Aiden. No big deal. We all got over it. Right?" More of that stubborn determination had her chin jutting out. "We're all grown-ups and can handle whatever. But what I'd really like right now is a shower and a change of clothes."

He stood there, mute, for a few seconds that felt like they stretched out for minutes. Instead of mounting a defense like he would've done ten years ago, he took her hand in his, linked their fingers, and then led her inside the house.

Once inside, he heard noises coming from the kitchen. The place was lively, unlike any time during his childhood. T.J. had always insisted that rowdy boys be sent outside. And, honestly, that's where Aiden had spent most of his time anyway. Outside in the barn. Anywhere was better than being in the same room with his father.

He smiled at Chloe, shoving those heavy thoughts aside. Children's laughter echoed down the hall. From the sounds of it, there were half a dozen Rugrats in there. "You sure you're ready for this?"

His attempt to lighten the mood failed miserably. Chloe was having none of it. He deserved the cold shoulder he was getting. He'd had that coming for a long time now that he really thought about it.

Back then, he'd convinced himself that he was doing her a favor by breaking contact. Was it really for her, though? Or had he shoved her into that same category as his family? Too painful to stay in contact with?

"I can handle anything, Aiden."

10

A house full of babies wasn't something he'd ever in a million years thought he would see at Quinnland Ranch. There was no amount of preparation possible to walk into the kitchen and see three highchairs pushed up against the dining table with nuggets in them happily eating.

Aiden had no idea what ages kids were based on the way they looked. A few of his employees had brought their kiddos to the office every once in a while. But it was too dangerous on a construction site to have the little tykes around, so his interaction with people shorter than two-and-a-half-feet tall was limited, to say the least. These little nuggets sat happily picking up what looked like cereal bits off their tray tables and seemed to find great amusement in trying to find their own mouths.

Gina Anderson...now Gina Quinn, sat next to one of the little tykes. Aiden's older brother, Isaac, was in the process of adopting the little girl named Everly. Marianne's back was turned and she must not have heard them come in. She stood at the sink and she was in the middle of a sentence when she must've realized new people were in the room. She gave a quick glance and then performed one hell of a double take.

Clutching her chest, he could hear her gasp from across the room. "Is that you, Aiden Quinn?"

"In the flesh." He was grateful that she seemed content to leave it at that and not bring up the fact that he hadn't been back to see her in ten years. He'd been sure to send her presents every Christmas and birthday, doing his level best to show his gratitude for all the years she loved, guided, and basically put up with him as a kid.

He heard a sniffle as she crossed the room and gave them both a big hug.

"Chloe Brighton, it's so good to see you again." Marianne had the kind of natural warmth that made people want to stand just a little bit closer to her on a cold day.

"You, too, Marianne." Chloe sounded a little choked up and he figured being back here probably brought up a lot of memories for her. Aiden hoped they were good.

Aiden squeezed Chloe's hand for support as Gina greeted them both. He remembered her from school, she'd been in Isaac's grade. It was surreal to see people he hadn't seen or thought of in years in the house where he'd grown up. "I've heard Everly is a sweet kid. My brother's lucky to have you both in his life."

"Thank you, Aiden." Gina glanced from him to Chloe. "Do you need anything?"

"Not unless you have an extra set of clothes you don't mind letting me borrow." Chloe's attempt at humor was met with a sincere nod.

"Actually, I do. If you're serious, you look to be about my same size. I'd be happy to lend you an entire outfit."

"That's actually very kind of you, Gina. I will take you up on that."

Gina looked toward Marianne, who was already nodding and smiling. "Go on. You know it's a joy for me to get to watch Everly."

"I'll be right back." Gina's smile was ear-to-ear and Aiden had never seen her happier. It was beyond him how anyone could have a little child who kept them up all night and still be smiling the next day. The cute little nuggets must have some special power. Mostly, Aiden heard men on the job groaning for how little sleep they got.

"Is that coffee I smell, Marianne?"

"You sit right down, Aiden. I'll get a cup. I heard word you might be coming home." Marianne looked to Chloe. "Can I get coffee for you? Are you hungry?"

Considering Chloe's stomach had just growled, he figured Marianne's question was answered.

"A shower and a toothbrush sound amazing right now. Is there any chance I can take a rain check on that breakfast and coffee until I get cleaned off and feel human again?" Chloe asked.

"Of course," Marianne stated.

"I can get my own coffee, Marianne. You have your hands full with these little nuggets. I'll get Chloe set up in my old room, so she can take a shower and then I'll be right back." The last thing he needed was the naked, sexy image of Chloe in his shower. So, he tried to set those thoughts aside. *Good luck with that, Quinn.*

Aiden linked his and Chloe's fingers as he made his way into the east wing that had housed him and his two brothers. Eli's room used to be the one next door to Noah's that was located up the stairs from off the kitchen. The twins had been down the hall opposite each other. The rest of the boys housed on the other side of the house. But they'd spent more time near Noah, Eli, and the twins' rooms than in their own spaces.

The same pictures lined the hallway. Remnants of a time when he'd had a mother. To be fair, Marianne had more than fit the bill and he was grateful as all get out for her influence in his life. He couldn't imagine what would've become of him or his brothers without her. Anything good inside them was instilled by Marianne.

Stepping into his room was like walking into a time capsule. It was the same as he'd left it ten years ago. There was a king-sized bed up against one wall. Two chairs nestled on either side of a large window with a small table in between. A dresser and a study desk rounded out the decor. He couldn't help but muse the study desk had been wishful thinking on Marianne's part. Aiden was never one to stay up late studying. He did enough to get by and stay on the football team, his respite from being chained to a tractor.

"I literally don't think one thing has changed in your room."

Chloe pointed to the adjacent bathroom. "Why do I have a sneaky suspicion the place is ready, complete with fresh towels, soap, and shampoo?"

"Because you've met Marianne. She'd make a Boy Scout look unprepared. That woman is always ready." He chuckled and it felt good to laugh with Chloe again. They needed to talk about what had happened in the parking lot in front of Casa Grande. But not now. "Are you okay in here by yourself or do want me to stay?"

The look she shot him said her thoughts had dropped to the gutter. "I think I can bathe myself, Aiden."

That really made him chuckle. "I should've known. And for the record, I wasn't talking about helping you in the shower. Although, if that's ever on the table..."

This time, she broke into a small smile. "I'll keep it in mind, Quinn. You know, in case there's a zombie apocalypse and there are no available living men left on the planet."

Ouch. He knew she was joking, but there was something in her words that really hit him, even if her good-natured teasing was one of the many qualities he loved in Chloe.

"In that case, I'll be down in the kitchen if you need me." He liked that she felt safe in his family's home. He wasn't sure where she stood after what she'd been through last night, and he wouldn't blame her one bit if she needed a body present in the room with her at all times.

Since she was okay, he figured this might be a good time to speak to Marianne alone in the kitchen. When he returned, Gina was there with a pile of folded clothes in her hands.

"I wasn't sure what she would need or what she liked or how long she would be here, so I gave her a lot of options." Gina smiled as she handed over the offering.

"This is very generous of you. I know Chloe will appreciate it and I'm thankful you went out of your way to make her feel welcome. She's been through a lot in the past few days and I'm sure it means a lot to her to feel so welcomed. That goes for you, too, Marianne."

Both women waved him off like it was nothing but it was everything.

It was everything he'd missed the past ten years by cutting himself off from his family. It was everything he forgot that he needed. It was everything he realized he wanted. Family. *His* family. The thought that there were so many new additions and the family was growing every day made him realize just how much the ranch seemed to be changing.

"I'll take those off your hands." Aiden jogged back to his room, stopping when he heard the shower running. Rather than disturb her or catch her off guard, he set the offering on the bed. And then he headed back downstairs.

No longer alone with Marianne, Aiden fixed himself a cup of coffee.

"How about that breakfast now?" she asked.

"I don't mind waiting for Chloe so she doesn't have to eat alone." The sweet look Marianne and Gina shot him caused him to backpedal real fast. "Before you get any ideas, it's not like that between me and Chloe. We go way back, as you of all people know, Marianne." He could understand why Gina might not realize the two had only ever been friends since they were not in the same class, but Marianne should know better.

"The two of them used to be everywhere around school together," Gina said. He'd seen her and his brother, Isaac, together a lot, too. And he never was sure what had happened between them except that Isaac had gone into the military and he thought Gina had moved to Dallas. He couldn't be certain. Back then, Aiden had been caught up in his own life and even though any one of his brothers could depend on him in a heartbeat, they didn't exactly know each other's day-to-day. In part, because they were too busy working the ranch or playing sports.

Aiden didn't mind, though. It had been better than being near his father, and he credited his work ethic with the discipline that had been instilled in him by the man. Between the ranch and sports, Aiden hadn't exactly had a lot of time to get into trouble.

"So, how has T.J. been doing?" He purposely left his question vague.

Marianne turned toward the sink. "I know he'll be happy to see you."

"And he's feeling okay?"

"Why? What have you heard?" The dish must've slipped out of her hands because it collided with the porcelain sink.

"That he's practically on vacation these days. He doesn't go to the meetings he set up at four a.m. and he can be found in his pajamas in the kitchen at seven-thirty in the morning. Odd behavior if you ask me."

Marianne made a phhh sound. "I don't know. It sounds like someone who isn't a kid anymore. Maybe he wants to enjoy more of his life instead of spending dusk to dawn working."

"Since when has ranching ever been work for T.J. Quinn?" This place was his life and he'd spent it building Quinnland into a successful, multimillion-dollar business. One that was his legacy. He'd built it from the ground up and he wasn't the kind of person to sit outside in his swim trunks and sip beer in a lawn chair for relaxation.

Marianne didn't respond. It was the first time in Aiden's life his instincts said she wasn't telling him something.

TWO WORDS CAME to Chloe while she was in the shower. *Cover up.* The words sounded off in her head, spoken by a male voice with an accent. The details were fuzzy. Her mind buzzed. She finished washing and quickly toweled off, and then it came to her. The guy had had a Cajun accent. After locating clothes folded on the bed, she quickly dressed and then headed downstairs.

Aiden was seated at the table and voices were a low hum as Chloe entered the room. Gina attended to her daughter. Aiden's eyes immediately flew to Chloe as she walked inside.

"I remembered something. It may be nothing. Two words came to me with a male voice while I was in the shower. 'Cover up.' I don't know why I remember it, but I feel like it's probably from the accident."

"Griff needs to know this." Aiden took out his phone and sent a text. She was grateful he didn't ask her for more details because it was all she had. She hoped it would help in some small way. Dr. Hill had mentioned that she could regain part, all or none of her memories from last night.

Aiden's phone buzzed, no doubt a response from Griff. He studied the screen. "He's actually on his way over to talk to you right now. Said he would be here in the next fifteen- to twenty minutes."

"Did he say why?" Chloe's stomach was a twist of knots.

"No."

"Do you think he has news about my brother?" Her words came out in a rush and her heart pounded.

Aiden's expression turned serious. "I don't think so. He would've said something if there was news about Nicholas."

Marianne had gone back to work on the dishes in the sink and Gina was preoccupied with her daughter and Eli's munchkins, but Chloe figured the two were giving her and Aiden privacy in their conversation. "What do you think the voice in my head means?"

Aiden studied his coffee mug for a long moment. "Well, I definitely think you remembered something and that's always a good thing. Griff might have a better context for it than I do. This voice? Did it seem familiar to you at all?"

"That part is a little fuzzy. It kind of sounded like it was in a tunnel." She could feel her shoulders deflate. The rejuvenation brought on by the shower short-lived. Chloe also had to face the possibility that an old memory had gotten jumbled up with the recent one. Dr. Hill had also explained that wires could get crossed as disappointing as that could be under the circumstances. She desperately wanted to remember something to help the investigation move forward. Chloe also figured the desperation could cause her to think she heard something when she didn't.

"How about some breakfast?" Marianne turned from the sink. "Food won't solve everything, but I've always found it impossible to think straight on an empty stomach."

"Thank you, but I'm not sure I could hold anything down." On second thought, Chloe really needed a cup of coffee about now and it was probably a bad idea to put caffeine on an empty stomach. "Actually, do you have yogurt?"

Aiden shot a look because she'd joked one too many times about never becoming one of those people who only ate yogurt for breakfast instead of bacon and eggs, and now she was one of them.

"Coming right up," Marianne said.

"I can get it. You don't have to go out of your way." Chloe was already standing near the fridge.

"No. You're a guest. Please, sit down and let me get you some yogurt. Do you have a specific flavor in mind?"

"Blueberry? But I'd take anything you have. I just want to get something on my stomach before..." She diverted her gaze to Aiden's coffee cup. "Caffeine."

He was up and standing in a heartbeat moving toward what she figured was the coffee maker. She would argue with him and tell him that she could get her own coffee, but he'd just wave her off. And after standing in the shower, she needed to sit down anyway. She'd had to protect the back of her head from water, but being clean felt amazing. Her stomach chose that time to revolt, making gurgling noises to let the whole world know she was hungrier than she realized.

Marianne walked over and set a blueberry yogurt and a spoon on a plate in front of Chloe. "Thank you so much."

Afterward, she returned to the fridge and pulled out a dish before she started heating it. The smells were amazing and after Chloe managed to get down a few bites of yogurt her stomach calmed down enough to think about eating something more substantial.

The skillet Marianne brought to the table had potatoes, eggs, bell peppers, and what looked like spinach cooked and ready to go. She set the skillet in between Chloe and Aiden with a spatula, two small plates, and forks.

"I thought maybe you could take a few bites." It had been a very long time since anyone had tried to mother Chloe. She'd almost forgotten what it was like to have people who cared about her until seeing Aiden again.

"Thank you. This is amazing."

Aiden put food on the plates and she could get used to him serving her breakfast, she mused.

The coffee was amazing. Chloe got down a few sips and started to feel half human again. She tried to think more about the words, the voices. Those details were out of reach. In fact, the voices were already distant.

She realized she was white-knuckling her coffee mug when she followed Aiden's gaze to her fingers. Taking in a slow, deep breath, she set the mug on the table. Nothing else turned up in her thoughts, so she took a few more bites of food.

The front door opened and she could hear Griff's radio squawking. The sound grew as he walked toward the kitchen. By the time he entered the room, her heart was in her throat, thumping wildly.

He gave a quick greeting to everyone before taking a seat at the table and handing over the purse and phone he'd brought in.

"Would you like a cup of coffee?" Marianne already had an empty mug in hand.

"I can't stay long enough to drink it but thank you anyway." He clasped his hands together and put his elbows on the table. "I got a hit on FoxyLady1234. The person your brother was communicating with online. *His* name is Kees Otilio and we traced his address to Shreveport."

"The voice I heard in my head had a Cajun accent."

"Aiden mentioned that in his text. I have a deputy on his way to interview Otilio and get a sense of where he was last night. Did your brother ever speak to you about the person he'd been interacting with online?"

"No. He never mentioned that he was potentially seeing someone." She locked gazes with Griff. "My brother would've believed that the person he was interacting with was a woman, not a man. I have no reason to question his sexuality."

Of course, any person who would lie about their identity was most likely up to no good. It was possible that her brother could've gotten caught up in something he didn't know about or understand and then by the time he figured it out, it could've been too late. Scenarios started running through her mind. Nicholas might've agreed to meet this person, wanting to get to know them better before he mentioned anything to Chloe. She could see where Nicholas wouldn't want to bring that up before he was certain this wasn't going to be another Becca situation.

One time, Chloe got on a dating site and she didn't mention it to anyone. The date had been a bust. The guy had been creepy. It might've just been one bad experience, but she took that as a sign to meet people the old-fashioned way, face-to-face.

Or, in her case, she'd spent most of her Friday nights doing laundry and then treating herself to a good book, preferring to spend the time alone versus waste it with someone who couldn't stir the kind of feelings Aiden had. After hanging around with Aiden Quinn for the better part of her life, she'd been ruined for normal men.

Marianne and Gina scooped the babies out of their highchairs before excusing themselves.

"Don't leave on my account." Griff explained he couldn't stay for long.

"It's time for these little lovebugs to go to the playroom and get some exercise." Marianne beamed.

Aiden leaned back in his seat. "What playroom?"

"The room that used to be your father's office."

Any other time, the look of confusion on Aiden's face would be priceless. Chloe didn't have time to think about it before another scenario ran through her mind involving Nicholas. Her brother might have agreed to meet this online person and when a man showed up, Nicholas might've told the guy he wasn't into that sort of thing. This person might have felt rejected and a fight could have ensued.

Nicholas would never have judged someone harshly for their dating preferences, but he wouldn't have taken too kindly to being lied to. His temper was something he was planning to work on in counseling.

But a person who entered a relationship with deception would not have had pure intentions. And, although Chloe wouldn't exactly call her brother helpless, he wasn't in the best state of mind or physical condition, either.

Again, the thought struck. Who would want to hurt Nicholas? As far as she knew, he didn't owe anyone money. All signs recently were pointing toward him starting to get his act together. He seemed to be accepting a new life with his disabilities and seeing a future.

Had he been telling her what she wanted to hear so she wouldn't worry about him so much?

11

"I keep going back to the theory that he would've been robbed." Nicholas's wallet was on his nightstand and there were still a few dollars in there. His credit cards and his ATM card were tucked in their slots. His bank account was intact and there'd been no suspicious activity that Chloe had picked up on when she'd glanced at his transactions. Nothing had stood out to her. Money couldn't have been the motive unless her brother had been robbed and murdered for less than a hundred dollars.

"Isn't it strange that nothing was taken from my brother's place? I mean, if he met up with someone online, wouldn't they want to take something from him? I mean, I'm just thinking out loud here, but I find it hard to believe somebody would hurt him for no reason," she couldn't bring herself to say the word *murder* out loud, "and then leave all his possessions behind. Also, the fact that Zeus didn't protect my brother is not something I can fathom. If someone had come to Nicholas's house and tried to be aggressive, Zeus would have guarded him the way he was guarding me when you found me."

"I agree that it's strange there was money in Nicholas's wallet and no obvious signs of robbery. Keep in mind, this was set up to look like your brother took his own life."

Those words weren't exactly reassuring. "What makes you think you'll find something in Shreveport? What was the nature of my brother's relationship with FoxyLady1234?"

"Their exchanges were of a personal nature. It's my belief that Nicholas thought he was connecting with and talking to a woman."

"And no one has attempted to steal his identity or done anything that you know of?"

Griff shook his head. "That's where we stand. I figured it was a shot in the dark that you would know who the online person was, but it was one worth taking."

"Thank you for following up on every possible lead in this case and for not giving up. Most law enforcement officers would probably call me crazy and close the file on my brother. It means a lot to me that you haven't done that."

"Just doing my job." Part of that was probably true, she suspected. However, Griff's reputation as one of the best sheriffs in Texas was well-deserved after seeing him in action.

He pushed back from the table and stood. "If anything else comes to mind, and I mean anything, no matter how small or insignificant it might seem, you already have my number. Reach out. Okay?"

"Will do." Chloe tried not to let all the wind be knocked out of her sails at once. But this was the fourth day that her brother had been missing. His dog had turned up. The neighbor had said Zeus had been thirsty, hungry, and exhausted. The heat from being outside for three days with his thick fur had drained a lot of his energy. The thought her brother could be out there somewhere, alone, needing her was a knife stab. "He doesn't have his medication. The bottles were in his kitchen cabinet, full."

"Nicholas was a good soldier from what I hear and that means he's tough." Aiden's statements sat in the air. Chloe knew without a doubt that her brother had been a great soldier. And that was another reason she was having a hard time buying the fact that he'd been tricked by someone who'd had to have convinced Nicholas to share his address, so they could come over in the first place. Then again, maybe having Zeus had given him a false sense of security.

Her brother had been secretive about a lot of aspects of his life. In truth, as much as she wanted to stand high and mighty on the fact that she knew her brother, she hadn't known about Levi Amon until Griff had mentioned him. She hadn't known about a possible internet relationship. He'd hid the fact that he'd been in contact with their cousin.

Chloe had a thought. Her brother might not have been confiding in her one hundred percent, but he had been opening up to his sponsor. At least about wanting help to deal with his dependency on pain meds. "I just had a thought. It's possible that my brother was talking to his sponsor about this new relationship."

"Kingston Herbert? The guy from earlier today?"

"Yes. He's the one. I'm just thinking that maybe my brother was willing to open up and talk to another guy. He might not be so comfortable telling his sister that he was trying to meet women online."

"If you follow along with that thinking, and I believe you're on to something here, this online person might've been in another relationship. Money isn't the only motive for murder. Crimes of passion are a sad but everyday reality in the world."

Chloe stood and started pacing. "A heat of the moment crime?"

"That's the idea."

A couple more steps and Chloe had to grip the island to stop from falling. Aiden was on his feet and to her side in a nanosecond.

"What is it? What happened?" His concern was outlined in the slashes in his forehead.

"I got a little bit lightheaded is all." She started to try to make up an excuse but one look at Aiden said it was useless. She wasn't going to be able to pull the wool over his eyes even though she was trying to convince herself that she was about to tell him the truth and not just make up a random excuse.

"I'm not talking about last night because I know you basically got in a few hours in total from naps here and there. But since this whole thing went down, how much sleep have you really had?"

"Not much." There was really no point in trying to candy coat the situation. His look of compassion said he would be doing the same thing—working himself to the bone to find answers. She knew how close he was to his family and his brothers at one time and, judging from the way they'd all rallied around him now, they still had each other's backs. If anything happened to one of them, not one of them would rest until answers had been found. Their dedication and loyalty to one another was another of many admirable traits shared by the Quinn brothers.

"How about this...we take this discussion to my room where there's a soft bed? We can still talk and bounce around ideas while you're curled up under the covers. I'll bring my laptop and we can discuss the case as long as you want." He waited for her to answer. The offer had merit and was tempting.

"I'm not gonna lie, part of me feels like I should be out there, searching. I just have no idea where to look for him anymore."

"I'm guessing you covered all his usual haunts?" Before Aiden could finish his sentence, Chloe was already nodding. "That was a given. You said that a neighbor found Zeus. Everyone in town is aware of your brother's situation. Right?"

"I mean, kind of. I've been talking to business owners and putting up Missing Person flyers. I don't think anyone realizes that he could still be alive or that he didn't do this to himself. I know I can't prove that part except that I know in my heart he is not capable of taking his own life." Aiden's suggestion to go upstairs and lie down was beginning to take on more importance as another round of light-headedness hit. She gave herself a minute to calm her racing pulse. "Speaking of my brother, have we heard any word on Zeus's condition today?"

Aiden pulled his cell phone and showed her the screen. "I meant to mention this. A message came while you were in the shower."

She read the screen and relief was cold water on a hot day. Zeus was doing well. Thank heaven for small miracles. "I need to think about trying to get him home to Austin with me."

"Why Austin?"

"Where else am I going to take him? I can't stay in my family's home. Not after what happened to Nicholas. I've been making the drive back and forth every day because I can't sleep there."

"I can have Michael bring him here as soon as he's ready. There's plenty of room at the ranch and you need him close by right now. Plus, if we need to take off there's always someone here to look after him. We can introduce him to Callie."

"Your brother still has her?" She remembered when the border collie was just a puppy. Such a sweet girl.

There was no way Chloe would argue or look this gift horse in the mouth. If Aiden was offering to let Zeus come stay at the ranch while she was there, she wouldn't argue. Instead, she nodded and then pushed up to her tiptoes and gave him a peck on the cheek.

"Thank you, Aiden. I don't know how I'll ever be able to repay you for everything you're doing for me."

"You'd do the same for me, Chloe." He was spot on. She would've done anything for him, would still do anything for him. Saying that she would do it because of their history was true. Saying that she would do it for their friendship was also true. Realizing that the only time her world had righted itself was in the time since he'd shown back up was truer than she wanted to admit to herself.

"Rest is probably a good idea as long as we keep throwing around ideas." Even the half cup of coffee she'd down didn't begin to make a dent in the exhaustion she felt. She'd been running on adrenaline and very little food for four solid days. It was bound to catch up to her at some point.

"After you." Aiden swept his hand out like he was presenting the way. "And I'll send a text to Michael and see if he can bring Zeus to the ranch. He'll be happier here than he will be at Michael's office. And, besides, as protective as that animal was over you, I think he needs to be around you right now until we find Nicholas."

Those last four words spoken out loud provided a burst of hope that, somehow, Nicholas was still alive.

Upstairs, she made Aiden look the other way and she changed into a T-shirt and a pair of pajama bottoms that Gina had provided. Chloe then slipped under the covers.

Aiden stretched out his legs and then his arms, and she had to force her gaze away from his strong back. "I'll be right back after I grab a quick shower."

Chloe leaned her head on the pillow and closed her eyes. She must've dozed off because she woke to the feeling of something heavy suddenly on the bed.

Blinking open blurry eyes, one word burst from her lips. "Zeus."

SEEING Chloe's reaction to Zeus brought a smile to Aiden's lips. By the time he came out of the shower an hour ago, she'd been asleep, lightly snoring. He hadn't wanted to disturb her, so instead, he'd pulled out a notepad and written down everything he knew about the case. Marianne would've been proud because it had been the first time he'd used that desk she had insisted go in his room for studying.

Aiden had opened his laptop next and done a little research on Levi Amon's group, known as The Anarchists. Amon had served in the military and had been dishonorably discharged. He was a known entity, angry at the government, and considered dangerous. The best that Aiden could tell, his members spread from Austin into Louisiana. The guy was trouble with a capital T. No doubt about that. But a murderer?

It seemed like a good time to remind himself that a body had not been found. It was next to impossible to prove a murder had been committed when there was no body. Aiden ruled out the possibility of Nicholas committing suicide. The information he learned from Chloe at the hospital about the blood splatter in the kitchen caused reasonable doubt.

Going down this path with Amon, Aiden had to consider what the guy's motive would have been.

His thoughts shifted to the possibility that when Nicholas had returned home, angry at the world and in the same emotional state toward the military and the government as Amon, the two could've easily hooked up. But what would their connection be? Aiden circled the question. It was one he wanted to ask Griff. The complication there was that Griff had an obligation not to give out information about an ongoing case. Certainly, Chloe deserves to know the status of where things stood in her brother's investigation. But there was protocol to consider.

It wouldn't look good for Nicholas to be involved with an anti-government group. In his angered state, he could've been influenced into signing up. Amon could've shown Nicholas how the organization ran. And then, say, Nicholas started getting his head screwed back on straight, decided that he didn't want to be part of Amon's group, after all. Playing out the scenario, Amon might not have been so thrilled about one of his trusted cohort's decision to back out. In fact, Amon could very well see the move as an outright betrayal.

However, would he risk the entire organization to get revenge on one person? Granted, it wouldn't be the first time something like this had happened. It just seemed risky for an organization's leader. The possibility Amon could've trusted Nicholas with information that would blow the organization wide open if it made the light of day struck Aiden. It would have been a plausible motive for murder. For Nicholas's sake as well as Chloe's, Aiden prayed that wasn't the scenario playing out here because that meant they were looking for a body.

But then why target Chloe?

Maybe she'd been getting too close to figuring out the truth for Amon's comfort. It was plausible, but a stretch.

The other possibility was that Nicholas had something Amon wanted. It was the only reason a kidnapping situation seemed reasonable. In that case, Amon could and would get rid of Nicholas the minute he didn't need him anymore.

Aiden couldn't imagine having to deliver that news to Chloe. Looking at her now, seeing the way her face lit up with Zeus caused a burst of pride. The fact the dog's tail was wagging like crazy didn't hurt matters. As those two continued to get reacquainted, Aiden went back to his notepad. He circled Amon's name and then moved on to the next. Jefferson Collier.

Jefferson had ties to the community. Based on Chloe's assessment of the guy, he was trouble. Whether people knew that or not remained to be seen. His most damning evidence was the fact that he'd been sneaking around to see Nicholas and had visited Hattie at the library specifically to learn more about inheritance. If both Nicholas and Chloe died, as much as Aiden didn't want to think about the possibility, Jefferson was the most likely heir to the Brighton family home and property. He had to know there would be some kind of investigation and his conversation with Hattie would be likely to come up.

Then again, the man might not be that bright. Aiden didn't know Jefferson personally. And, frankly, Aiden had been too busy in high school to focus on anyone outside his circle. But based on what Chloe said about her cousin, Aiden didn't like him. Jefferson didn't have a Cajun accent. Aiden had to consider that.

But then Aiden wasn't sure how much stock he should put in Chloe's memory. Trauma to the brain was a tricky thing. And even if her memory could be counted on, surely, Jefferson wouldn't be stupid enough to attack his cousins personally. He could know someone who knew someone. Or Jefferson could have an association with a person on the wrong side of the law.

Still, Aiden had to wonder about the lack of common sense it would take to ask the town librarian questions about inheritance right before trying to get rid of his cousins. Then again, Jefferson had been careful not to check out any books. He'd only asked Hattie what she knew. There was no paper trail. Without a body, there couldn't be a murder. And, Chloe's car crash had been staged to look like it had been an accident. What law enforcement agency would investigate a suicide and a car crash? In fact, most folks in town would look at the fact Chloe had lost her parents at a young age, then her brother to suicide and her death from a car crash would have been chalked up to bad luck. Since bad things tended to happen in threes, many folks would write off the family as unlucky.

Aiden circled Jefferson Collier's name as a possible suspect. Also,

Aiden took note of the two words Chloe remembered hearing. *Cover up.* Those words could apply to Amon as well as Jefferson.

Moving on to the budding internet relationship. Kees Otilio. There was an obvious connection to Shreveport. Chloe wouldn't know this person if she was in the same room with him. The fact that Otilio had been lying about his identity to Nicholas put him at the top of Aiden's suspects' list. It was a no-brainer to circle his name as a suspect.

Without knowing much else about the interactions between Nicholas and Kees, it was difficult to establish a motive. The obvious ones were that Nicholas believed he was having intimate conversations with a woman and was mortified when he decided to take the next step and meet the person on the other end of the computer, only to find out he'd been talking to a man.

Those kinds of cases were all over the news. A fight could have ensued. Things could've gotten out of hand. Thereby, the blood splatter. Killing Nicholas could've been an accident. Kees might have panicked and did away with the body out of panic or fear of backlash. He could come from any walk of life. He could be married. Being outed in this way could've shattered his life. That was one reason people hid their identities in these situations. They had a lot to lose if revealed in their 'other' life.

Nicholas would've known someone was coming over if he'd invited them. Thereby, he would've made arrangements for Zeus, and even welcomed Kees into his home. Zeus would've followed Nicholas's lead, allowing the stranger access without much protest. He could've been let outside when the fight took place. Otherwise, Aiden had no doubt the dog would've intervened.

That didn't exactly explain a suicide note in Nicholas's handwriting. Unless, of course, Kees found a few notes or something with Nicholas's handwriting on it and mimicked it perfectly.

Considering this event—be it murder or kidnapping—had occurred four days ago, forensics was still processing the blood splatter. It wasn't like on television where everything happened with the snap of a finger. The handwriting analysis could be done sooner if an expert was available. No doubt, Griff would've tapped into his resources.

The note had been dated four days ago. Zeus had been missing that long as far as anyone could tell. But it had taken at least a day for Chloe to get worried enough to alert Griff to do the wellness check.

Three suspects could've already been familiar with Zeus. The fourth, Kees from the internet, could've been invited inside Nicholas's house.

In fact, Nicholas might not have known Kees was a man until the relationship turned physical. Aiden really wanted to find out who was responsible, partly for Nicholas, but also because he realized how much he needed Chloe to be safe again.

12

"It's so good to see this guy again."

Zeus had settled down beside Chloe, snuggled against her leg. Aiden smiled, happy that he could provide at least a little comfort.

"He seems pretty happy to see you, too."

Chloe practically beamed back at him. It was in that moment he realized just how much he missed her.

"You've been quiet. What are you thinking about?" she asked.

Where did he even start? He picked up his pad of paper and move beside her on the bed. Zeus's head popped up and emitted a low growl.

"It's okay, boy." Chloe's soothing tone calmed the animal. Zeus was going to have to get used to Aiden being around at some point. He was already starting to question whether or not he could run his business from Gunner. Possibly even build an office downtown or rent one of the unoccupied spaces; it seemed there was always real estate readily available in a small town. Aiden was already thinking of the jobs he could create for the community in addition to the ones he'd created in Colorado.

He couldn't help but wonder if he and Chloe could pick up their friendship where they left off years ago. She lived in Austin now. However, her brother—God willing—would return to their family home safe and sound. She would come here to visit and maybe she and Aiden could meet up for lunch or hang out at the lake once in a while like old times.

There was no way Aiden could think about this scenario ending with Nicholas gone. And now that he had Chloe back in his life, he had to figure out a way to make it more permanent again.

"Zeus doesn't seem to be my biggest fan, but I hope in time he'll get used to me." Aiden tested the waters with Chloe to see where her thoughts were about seeing him more often.

She didn't take the bait. Instead, she changed the subject altogether leaving him a little bit confused. "I'm sure he can't wait to be reunited with Nicholas." She didn't lift her gaze to look at Aiden. Maybe he'd been reading her the wrong way all this time. Maybe she was ready to move on from their friendship. That thought hurt more than Aiden wanted to admit.

"I've been going over the evidence in my mind. So far, I've written down someone with a Cajun accent is involved. I noted the words *cover up*. There was blood splatter that is unexplained by suicide. And then there's the note itself. You mentioned that Nicholas would never have apologized and based on what I knew of your brother, I would agree. And then there was the staged car crash. The convenient deer on the road. And we know whatever happened with Nicholas, the person would've had to get past Zeus."

Chloe nodded in agreement.

"We have four suspects." She cocked an eyebrow. "Stay with me for just a second on this."

"I'm all ears because I count three. Two if you don't include my cousin."

"I'm including him all right. In my mind, he has the most to gain. But I'm not sure we've stumbled onto the real motive yet. Like I said, four suspects. Jefferson Collier, Kees Otilio, Levi Amon, and Kingston Herbert." That last name got her attention all right.

"My brother's counselor? What would he have to gain by anything happening to my brother?"

"I included him on the list because he had access. He also has a Cajun accent. Whoever was in your brother's house, in his kitchen was most likely invited there. The blood splatter, at least in my thinking, means that your brother was surprised by someone. Being military, he would most likely only turn his back on someone he trusted. Kingston would know enough about the way your brother spoke to craft a suicide note. He could've even tricked your brother into writing it in the first place as part of 'therapy'. Staging the car crash is anyone's guess. We really don't have a lot of information about what happened there. And, again. Whoever took your brother for lack of a better term would've had to have gotten past Zeus. Which probably means the person had visited before. It could even be someone who'd gained Zeus's trust."

She sat still for a long moment, seeming to contemplate those words. "All of those are really good points and I probably missed all of them. I guess my question is...why? What would Kingston have to gain from hurting my brother?"

"That's the missing piece and the reason why there are three other names on my list. However, I think our best bet moving forward is to tackle each name one by one. It's probably not realistic for us to go to Shreveport and do our own investigation into Kees. Do you still have your brother's laptop?"

Chloe was shaking her head. "No. I turned that into Griff for evidence. And you already know from last night that he has mine."

"What about your brother's bank account and phone records? Do you have access to those?"

Those violet eyes of hers lit up. "That I can help you with. Can I use your laptop? And I'll probably need my phone because if I log on from a different system the bank will want to send me a verification code to input."

Aiden retrieved the items and brought them to her. He also snagged a pea-size piece of cooked bacon for Zeus, who didn't bother to take it until Chloe gave him permission. The animal was well trained. Caution would be part of that training. He also knew retired military service dogs were prone to biting, so he kept a safe distance deciding to sit on the other side of Chloe.

"Good boy." She stroked his fur and he lowered his head onto his front paws. She had a soothing effect on animals and people.

He showed her the pad of paper. She leaned back. "May I hold it?"

"Of course." Being this close to her caused her warm floral scent to invade his senses, stirring that place in his chest where his otherwise useless heart still beat.

"Jefferson is a bad influence. Dangerous? I'm not sure. But then who wants to think their cousin could've done something to their brother or try to hurt them?" She ran her finger over Levi's name. "He just seems dangerous."

"We already know that he is. People don't end up on a watchlist for no reason." Before Aiden finished his sentence, Chloe was already nodding.

"I don't like this guy." She pointed to Kees's name. Aiden couldn't argue there. "My brother seemed to really like his counselor. I feel like he was starting to open up more and more to Kingston. My brother was against the idea of talking to someone when he first got back. Kingston was the first person he opened up to and trusted."

They didn't know exactly how much Nicholas had told Kingston. Even though he was more of a sponsor then a true counselor, Aiden didn't figure the guy would tell them intimate details if Nicholas had shared them. And that was a big *if*.

Aiden had a brother as well as other friends who'd returned from the military who had gotten pretty damn good at covering their true feelings. Soldiers weren't used to asking for help when it came to dealing with their emotions or anything else for that matter. A soldier was someone the government called on to be the solution to a problem. It was ingrained in most every soldier that Aiden had ever known to keep his or her cards close to the chest when it came to emotions. They were great people and he was grateful for their service. But even outwardly strong men and women needed to lean on someone else sometimes. Aiden was just as guilty as the next person of shutting down his own feelings. Of moving on without taking the time to make it right.

"Okay, let me poke around my brother's finances and see if I can come up with anything." She set the notepad down and her fingers danced on the keyboard. Her cell phone dinged, and she checked the screen. She entered the verification code and pulled up Nicholas's account.

Aiden scooted beside her so they could share the screen.

"I'm not really seeing anything that causes any big red flags. Are you?" she asked.

He shook his head. "Nothing big. What are these charges?"

There was a series of hits to his ATM. Small amounts. Different amounts. Regular withdraws.

Chloe shrugged. "I'm not really sure why he would take out thirty dollars and then forty dollars. There's another one for sixty dollars and then another thirty. It keeps repeating. This would really add up over a month-long period. Let's total this up." She pulled up a calculator app and entered the amounts. She turned and looked at Aiden. "One thousand dollars."

"That's a very specific total."

"It sure is." Chloe wondered if it could be an admission fee to Levi's group. It was possible even though she highly doubted it that Levi had talked Nicholas into joining his anti-government mission. "I just wonder what it's for. I know my brother didn't have any need to take out that kind of money in a month for cash, considering he didn't really go anywhere. I brought food to him, especially in those early months when he first came home. Now, I always come on Sundays to take him to the grocery store and run any other errands he needs."

"I can't help but wonder why he would feel the need to be so secretive. Why not take out a thousand dollars if that's what you need?" Aiden was probably on the right track and she hated the fact her brother felt the need to hide things from her.

"I was usually with him. Or so I thought. Whoever was visiting him on a regular basis may have been taking him to the ATM machine. Someone had to have been coming over besides me. He would've known that I would've asked questions. When he first got back, I managed his account. He was slowly starting to take those things over and check back into life after not being really sure he wanted to be here for a while." Chloe realized how that sounded and especially considering there was a suicide note. "That didn't come out right."

"I knew what you meant. Your brother came home trying to figure things out again. He was going through a rough patch. He may have even talked about the possibility of ending his life or giving up. From everything I've ever heard or read, people who intend to take their own lives do it. They don't talk about what they're going through."

Aiden took her hand in his, causing electrical impulses to vibrate up her arm from the point of contact. "I hope Nicholas knows how lucky he is to have you. Not too many people would go out of their way to fight this hard, especially when someone was pushing them away. You are incredibly brave in case I haven't told you that lately."

He punctuated his complements with a tender kiss that released a dozen butterflies in her stomach and unleashed a tidal wave of want. She probably wasn't supposed to feel like this toward her best friend.

Nothing in her wanted him to stop kissing her. She gathered her strength and pulled back enough to say, "Aiden."

He froze and his lips were so close to hers it would be so easy to lean forward just a little bit, into them, into him. Her heart had been shattered the last time he left and that was after they'd only been best friends. She knew better than to want more and he probably wasn't even offering it anyway.

"I know what you're going to say. And, yes, this is probably a bad idea." His voice was a low rumble from deep in his chest. Sexy. Tempting. Irresistible.

The two of them sat there for a long moment, neither seemed

ready to move. Even Zeus appeared to have decided to take a chill pill when it came to Aiden being close to her. Chloe could only wish one of those magic pills was available for her when she went back to her life in Austin and he disappeared to Colorado again. There'd be no such medicine to help her pick up the pieces of her shattered heart. So, she forced herself to refocus on the computer and the pad of paper sitting next to her on the bed.

Aiden followed her lead even though it took him a minute to open his eyes. "Tell me what your brother was like when he first came home. Walk me through his moods, what you can remember him talking about."

"I can't count the number of weeks he'd stayed on the couch, unable to motivate himself enough to get up. After his fiancée broke off their engagement, he sank into an emotional pit. He'd sleep eighteen hours a day and had no desire to eat. He must've lost twenty pounds and was starting to waste away."

"Losing the person he thought he'd spend the rest of his life with had to have been a huge blow, especially after feeling like he'd lost so much already." Aiden couldn't have been more on point there. Her brother had shriveled up like a plant that had lost its water source after losing his fiancée.

"I took leave from my job for the first few weeks but couldn't take off much more than that after I ran out of vacation time and sick leave. My boss was great about everything but he could only let me off for so long before my lab would start falling apart. I'm the most senior person there and got promoted into management last year." Every weekend, she'd bring home enough food for half the week and then clean up the small house they'd inherited from their parents. It wasn't much and it wasn't Chloe's taste. She preferred Austin to living in Gunner where there were too many reminders of Aiden.

"It sounds like you were doing everything you could to help your brother." She wished she felt like she'd made an impact. Half the time she'd come home and he'd barely say two words to her. The other half he'd be so angry she wished he wouldn't talk. It was probably selfish to think that way but it was true.

"When he came home on his first leave, I hardly recognized him, if that makes sense."

Aiden nodded.

"He became so much more respectful and self-disciplined. When he'd stay at our parents' house the place would be spic and span when he left. Sheets folded on top of the bed where he'd slept. Those were good changes." She paused. "He started to become more serious about life, about his future. I was happy if I could get him to put away his own laundry in high school."

"Our house could've been boot camp when it came to household chores. T.J. made sure nothing was left out of place." Maybe she should've figured out how to instill some of that in her brother when he was younger. Her parents had left much of the household chores to her while they worked. With Nicholas being the baby, they all had spoiled him. Their mother used to joke with Chloe that if she didn't let him start making his own lunch he'd never eat when he went off to college.

"He never talked about what happened over there to cause him to lose part of his leg and his hand." All she knew was that the fresh-faced young man who'd signed up eagerly to serve his country had disappeared what felt like overnight. He'd been barely eighteen years old and a high school graduate when he'd signed up to serve in the U.S. Army.

"I can only imagine what it would be like to be in his place." Aiden shook his head and there was so much sympathy in his voice. "Staring down a future that he didn't recognize anymore."

At twenty-three, he'd medically boarded out due to the injury that had taken his right leg from the knee down and part of his left hand. His fiancée, Becca, had ended their relationship a few weeks after he'd come home. Until then, Chloe had thought he might come out of the difficult situation he was in.

"When Becca broke his heart, he hit rock bottom." Chloe didn't think it could get worse for her brother than when he first came home. Losing Becca had taken his pain to a whole new level. He'd retreated to a different place, a truly dark place.

"Understandable." Chloe would have to take his word for it. She would never let anyone get close enough to her to cause the kind of pain that would make a person become so depressed that sleeping away the days seemed like a better alternative to being awake. Too much lying in bed, asleep or being lazy, didn't do good things to her body. She'd grossly overslept one Saturday morning after a long week on her feet at the lab and woke up so stiff she had to take a long hot shower to bring her muscles back to life.

"That brings us to the point where I might have actually believed it if I'd gotten a call about my brother's well-being. I didn't know what to do to help him. So, I got desperate and called an old friend. Do you remember Ash Cage?"

"Hell, yeah, I remember him. I was living in Colorado when he medically boarded out from the military. Although, I didn't know it until he came through the other side of what he was dealing with. He got a dog by the name of Seven."

"That's right." A desperate Chloe had reached out to Ash Cage, praying he could spread around some of the magic that had saved him. "He helped me get my brother hooked up with the government agency in San Antonio responsible for the K-9 unit. Zeus had hit retirement years before his handler and was in need of a good home." She petted him. "He's older than most."

Aiden eyed Zeus with a warm smile. "I'm convinced animals have healing powers."

"I really wasn't sure how it would turn out. Taking on the responsibility of a dog is a lot. When I told Nicholas what I was thinking, he immediately perked up. It was like a light flipped on inside him. He would get up at six o'clock in the morning and take a shower. He got online and started reading up on how to help Zeus acclimate to the world outside of the only job he'd ever known." Nicholas had said that he needed to establish a routine and she'd been both proud and relieved to hear him taking charge of his life.

"Sounds like he rose to the occasion." Aiden had that right. Nicholas had knocked it out of the park.

"That's where the disconnect is for me. Life was looking up for him and he loved Zeus. He put himself on the list for a prosthetic fitting." Once Zeus arrived, her brother really started to shine. "Nicholas started a rigorous exercise routine that included training with Zeus in the backyard. He came up with a plan to wean himself off all the medications he'd been taking. And he'd mentioned making an appointment at the VA to talk to a therapist. He thanked me for everything I'd been doing for him."

So, no, she couldn't accept that her brother had written an apology before taking his own life and leaving the one bright spot— and it had been huge—in his life. His dog. "I know none of that is proof to an outsider that suicide was the last thing my brother would do right now. And I can't prove how I know. I just do."

"It's proof enough for me."

Chloe wiped away a rogue tear. She blinked blurry eyes. She thought back to her last conversation with Nicholas. He'd sounded upbeat. The depression that had been a heavy curtain over his once-bright personality seemed to be lifting. He'd started joking around again.

Seeing Nicholas happy again had distracted her from the fact that her boyfriend, Finn Docker, had broken up with her because she'd been spending all her time with her brother. He'd said that she wasn't fun anymore. Fun. Her brother was battling for his life and all Finn cared about was the fact she couldn't spend every weekend on Lake Travis on his new boat with him? Man, had she misjudged his character.

To be fair, she wasn't looking for a serious relationship when she'd started dating Finn. Their deal had been having fun together and she didn't do complicated anymore after her friendship with Aiden.

Where was her usual good sense when it came to the men she dated?

13

"It's safe to rule out suicide."

Aiden decided she should know where he stood on the case. A person who'd adopted a dog and was on the road to straightening up his life wasn't the right candidate for suicide. Whether they were looking for Nicholas alive or otherwise remained to be seen and he'd keep that part to himself. There was no sense adding to Chloe's burden and she had to know both scenarios were possible. Four days was a long time to be missing and law enforcement didn't seem close enough to figuring out who Nicholas might have been involved with and why, or what kind of trouble he could've gotten himself into.

"Thank you for believing me, Aiden. And for believing in Nicholas." She touched his hand and sent a firebolt up his arm. So much for keeping his attraction in check. But then, this was no ordinary attraction. This was Chloe.

Aiden had never let himself fall for his best friend before. He'd always kept his emotions in check even when they'd tried to run wild in high school. He could only imagine how great sex would be with a mind-body connection like the one they had. But she was injured and, besides, sex wasn't on the bargaining table right now nor would it be.

Still, after the few kisses they'd shared...his imagination and desire was taking on a life of its own.

"I remember what your brother was like growing up. I'm sure he went through a lot losing your parents so young. You went through a lot trying to make up for it. He was strong even for a kid in high school. Sounds like he hit a low after he came home, as many people do. There are so many ups and downs in life. A person's actions might change but character doesn't. The core of who we are is a constant. Your brother was a good person when I knew him before. He's a good person now." Aiden's mind really was spinning, though. "He might've gotten mixed up with trouble and it caught up to him before he realized what was going on."

"I think in the state he was in, it might have been a little easy to prey on him. My cousin is a jerk, but I distinctly remember hearing a Cajun accent. He's greedy, but there's no way my brother or myself would leave our parent's property to him."

"Is he your only living relative?"

"I guess he's the only one that I know of now that you mention it."

"Do either you or your brother have a will?" Even with the fact that Aiden owned a successful business, he didn't have one. Being so young and without a wife and kids, it never really crossed his mind that if something happened to him there could be a fight over his business. None of his brothers would want his money or company. There wasn't a greedy bone in any one of their bodies. Aiden believed he'd surrounded himself with good people at work. But when money or power came into play, things could change.

"Nicholas would have to speak for himself. He never mentioned anything about having one, though. I definitely don't." She shrugged. "Now that I think about it, it seems a little naïve not to have our wishes down on paper, should anything happen to either of us or both."

Aiden's cell buzzed, so he grabbed it and checked the screen. Zeus practically came off the bed for how high he jumped with the sudden noise while he'd been asleep. "I have a message from Griff. He's asking if we can come to his office."

Chloe immediately shifted the laptop off her lap as she said soothing words to Zeus. "I just need a minute to change and I'll be ready."

Aiden nodded to Chloe as he responded to the message, letting his cousin know they were on their way. He forced his eyes away from Chloe as she grabbed a jogging suit that Gina had let her borrow and then disappeared into the bathroom, Zeus right at her side.

She returned a couple minutes later with her hair brushed away from her face.

"Tell your shadow that he's welcome to come with us." Aiden couldn't help but smile at the loyalty Zeus was already displaying to Chloe. His skepticism of Aiden seemed to be slowly dissolving.

Grabbing keys from the top of his dresser and a pair of flip-flops for Chloe, Aiden led the procession down the stairs. His truck was parked in front right where he'd left it this morning. He unlocked and opened the passenger door first. Zeus immediately jumped inside and sniffed around before settling into the middle of the bench seat. Chloe waited patiently until Zeus settled and then climbed into the passenger side. She buckled in.

Traffic was light, so they made it to Griff's office in record time. Sherry, Griff's longtime secretary, welcomed them and led them immediately into Griff's office. The minute he saw them come in, he ended the call he was on and stood up.

"Your cousin is here, demanding to talk to me or one of my deputies. He says he has information about Nicholas's death." Griff flashed eyes at Chloe.

"If he knew something, why wouldn't he come forward sooner?" Chloe folded her arms across her chest as Griff's gaze bounced from Zeus to her. He seemed to realize they were going to be a package deal.

"His response to that question when I asked it was that he didn't realize Nicholas might've been murdered until what happened to you." If anyone asked Aiden, it sounded pretty far-fetched. He didn't trust Jefferson as far as he could throw him. Did that mean the guy was a murderer?

Chloe dropped her hands, balled her fists and placed them to either side of her hips. "It's good he could have this sudden epiphany once he realized I might've been hurt. Did it not dawn on him before?"

"I thought you might want to be in the watch room when he gives his statement." Griff paused for a brief second. "Also, I've asked your brother's sponsor to come in and give his statement. His name has come up a few times during the course of my investigation and I'd like to hear his opinion of what might've happened to Nicholas first-hand."

"My brother was taking money out of his bank account. I know you were looking at that information. He was taking out small deposits that added up to a thousand dollars in a month. Do you have any idea why?"

"We know that Levi Amon was in contact with Nicholas. The two knew each other from their service. As best as we can gather, Levi contacted your brother once he heard about Nicholas's situation and that he was out. Did you know Levi stayed with your brother for two weeks not long after your brother came home?"

DUMBFOUNDED WASN'T the right word for what Chloe felt. Betrayed. Now that was a word. She'd visited her brother regularly and cleaned the house. How could he hide there? She felt her hands fisted at her sides, so she crossed her arms over her chest to have something to do with them because right now even though she was one of the most nonviolent people around all she wanted to do was throw a punch at something. Where was a punching bag when she needed one?

"Nicholas allowed Levi Amon to stay in our parent's home?"

"That's right." An apologetic look crossed Griff's features.

Granted, Nicholas hadn't exactly lied to her about Levi Amon. She hadn't known to ask and he sure hadn't brought it up. So, technically, he hid his friend in their family home. "A man like Levi Amon seems like the kind of person who would make a lot of enemies."

"We're following up on all leads, chasing the evidence until we get answers."

"Why would my brother hide a dangerous known criminal in our home?" Chloe didn't realize she'd asked the question out loud until Aiden answered.

"Your brother might not have known that Amon had started this antigovernment group. Think about it, they served together in the military. Or at least, their paths crossed there. They most likely traded information and figured out that they lived in the same state and not that far away from each other. They decide to hook up state-side when their service was over, wish each other luck and move on. Happens all the time." It would certainly explain why her brother would bring danger to their doorstep. Chloe wanted to believe that Nicholas wouldn't have invited Levi to their hometown.

She looked to Griff for confirmation.

"It's entirely possible that Nicholas didn't know what he was getting into. Amon's issue with the government came toward the end of the service. We don't exactly know when the two met. To Aiden's point, though, Amon might've just shown up on Nicholas's doorstep and he might've asked to borrow money." It would be just like her brother to take him in no matter what.

"Servicemen form a bond similar to law enforcement. Those you serve with become your family. You depend on them to keep you alive as much as they depend on you," Griff added.

When he put it like that some of her anger abated. Nicholas wasn't the kind of person who would turn away someone in need, and especially not someone he felt a bond with. "Why hide it from me then?"

"Might not have been Nicholas's idea. Amon could've convinced Nicholas to keep quiet about him staying there." She could see her brother lending money to Levi Amon if he asked for it. The secrecy about it might not have been Nicholas's idea, but it made her feel like Levi Amon was guilty of something. Levi Amon may have tried to recruit Nicholas and when he failed, he might have done harm to her brother. Chloe didn't like that scenario one bit because it meant her brother was gone. She couldn't allow herself to go there. Hope was all she had left.

"When was the last time anyone saw Levi Amon?" she asked Griff. "You mentioned before that he moves around his headquarters." He seemed impossible to find let alone bring in for questioning.

"There were reports that he was here, staying with Nicholas. My contact said they always seem to be one step behind him, following his trail rather than being proactive."

That didn't sound encouraging. If Nicholas was alive and with someone like Levi Amon, he might be trying to find an opportunity to escape. She couldn't imagine her brother going off with him and leaving his dog behind. Of course, that would mean that her brother had gone willingly.

"If this Levi person stayed at the house, Zeus would have been familiar with him. He might've even been helping my brother care for him." She bent down to Zeus's level and looked into his eyes. If only he could talk. When the neighbor had corralled him into her yard and finally gotten a hold of Chloe, Zeus had been exhausted, hungry, and thirsty. There was no way Nicholas would allow that to happen. She could only pray that he wasn't with Levi Amon, and one of the other suspects worked out. For her money, the guy posing as a woman from the internet seemed to have a lot to lose if his identity had been revealed. He had an obvious motive for murder.

"Your cousin is waiting in the interview room. Are you ready for this?" As much as Chloe couldn't stand her cousin, she also couldn't imagine Jefferson trying to harm her or Nicholas. She was ready to hear what he had to say for himself.

A collective *yes* came from both her and Aiden.

"Is it okay if he comes with us?" Chloe motioned toward Zeus, who sat dutifully by her side.

"Wouldn't have it any other way." Griff led them down the hallway and to a room not much bigger than the size of a walk-in closet that had the lights dimmed.

There was a two-way mirror the size of a picture window that allowed her to see clearly into the interview room. Jefferson sat at a table that had chairs facing each other across the table. From her position, she could see his face clearly. Aiden stood behind her, placing his hands on her shoulders. It was all she could do not to lean back into his warmth.

Jefferson leaned forward, resting his elbows on the table in front of him. He looked directly at the two-way mirror and squinted. *Good luck figuring out who is watching*, Chloe thought.

Griff walked in, his demeanor calm and relaxed, in contrast to his tense expression only moments ago. The first thing he did was thank Jefferson for coming. The move was brilliant because her cousin's shoulders relaxed a little bit.

"It didn't seem too important at the time." Jefferson's gaze bounced from the mirror to Griff and back when he spoke. Zeus started pacing.

Chloe was certain she'd heard Aiden mutter the word *shifty* and she'd thought the same thing herself as she watched her cousin's actions. What was his plan? Kill her and then a few days or weeks later Nicholas's body would be found? The idea of hurting someone else for money sickened her. And yet it happened all the time according to the cop shows she occasionally watched on her day off.

She hugged her elbows into her chest, digging into her skin with her fingernails. Why an innocent person would show up to a search party and then contact the sheriff for a statement later on, puzzled her. Wouldn't people want to stay as far away from the investigation as possible? Wait until they were contacted for a statement rather than force themselves on the investigation? This was strange behavior even for Jefferson. He'd never once taken an interest in her or Nicholas's lives. The only time Jefferson seemed interested in his younger male cousin at all was when he needed someone to do his dirty work.

"What made you request this meeting?" Griff asked, his voice a sea of calm.

"As I said last night, this is my family. I want to be involved every step of the way." Zeus circled Chloe.

"Out of love and concern?"

"Would there be any other reason?" Chloe had to fight the urge to plant her palm on the mirror and call her cousin out as a liar. Where was Jefferson when Nicholas came home and needed help? As far as she knew their cousin hadn't once volunteered to run Nicholas to the doctor or the grocery.

Griff didn't respond. "You came here to tell me something..."

"Right." Jefferson made a show of rubbing the scruff on his chin as he leaned forward. "Nicky had a friend over a couple of times when I stopped by. He was secretive about it, and at first, I thought it might be a lady-friend."

Chloe wondered if he might be talking about Kees? A guy like Jefferson would have a field day with Nicholas being tricked and embarrassed.

"Did you ask him about who was there?" Griff took out a notepad and set it on the table. She took note that he didn't pull out a pen like he had when he was interviewing her. Did that mean he wasn't putting much stock in what Jefferson was saying?

"Not outright. The person rode a motorcycle, though." That didn't necessarily mean it was a man, but Chloe had observed it was more often than not in Gunner. "And he tucked it around the house like he was trying to hide it."

"Did you get a look at the plates?"

"I wished I had looking back. If I'd known then what I know now." He hung his head like he couldn't continue. "Let's just say I would've made note of the tags."

"Do you have a guess as to who the motorcycle belonged to?"

"I have no doubt. I saw him filling up the tank at the gas station a few days ago and it wasn't hard to put two-and-two together. The motorcycle rider was none other than Levi Amon."

14

"Did he just try to deflect blame?"

Aiden wasn't sure how to answer Chloe's question. Her muscles tensed underneath his hands at the mention of Amon's name.

"When did you see Mr. Amon at the gas station?" Griff's voice remained steady, like Jefferson hadn't just all-but accused a known anti-government leader of doing harm to Chloe's brother.

"Let's see now. It must've been Sunday, mid-day."

"He's lying through his teeth," Chloe said quietly and emphatically. "I was at the house with Nicholas all day. There's no way Levi Amon was there." She tried to calm her brother's dog, who was making low whining noises.

Aiden didn't need to work in law enforcement to hear the slight hesitation in Jefferson's voice when he gave the rough estimate of the time of day. All he said was, "I know." Those two words solicited a look from Chloe and a raised eyebrow. Again, he didn't need to depose witnesses for a living to realize she wondered how he knew. The question was written all over her face.

Griff nodded.

Whatever happened, it was clear more than one person was

involved. It would've been next to impossible for someone to act alone at the site of Chloe's so-called accident. Besides, after seeing her injuries it was clear that she'd been struck from behind. There would've had to of been another person around to deal with Zeus. Although considering he wasn't restrained in the seat, he might've been dazed and disoriented after impact. Still, based on Chloe's injuries it looked like she wasn't about to go down without a fight. The most likely scenario and the one that made him ball his fists involuntarily said that an accident was staged, Chloe was attacked and managed to get away.

Her death was supposed to look like a car crash. Again, whoever orchestrated this missed a few steps in the planning process. The person underestimated Chloe and was probably still angry that she was alive. Both her and Zeus had gotten away, possibly together. Or when he really thought about it, it was more likely that Zeus had found her in the woods.

So, technically, the person who had the Cajun accent wasn't necessarily the person who'd masterminded this whole crime. Aiden would bet good money that Cajun Accent was an accomplice.

Considering an attempt had been made on Chloe's life, Aiden wasn't super optimistic about Nicholas's chance of being alive. Losing the last of her family and her younger brother would devastate Chloe.

Aiden stared at the shifty family relative through the two-way mirror. Then there was Levi Amon to consider. Jefferson had just made a statement that he'd seen Amon in town the day before Nicholas disappeared.

"Did Levi Amon go inside the convenience store or pay at the pump?" Griff asked.

"He went inside." It would be easy enough to ask the gas clerk if he or she saw a person matching Amon's description on the day in question. In a bigger town, it would be laughable to ask a gas station attendant if he or she remembered customers. This was Gunner, a town where folks knew each other and businesses were family-owned. Very few people rode motorcycles; Trucks, Jeeps, and SUVs were far more common in these parts. Camera recordings were too grainy and most businesses didn't keep the files for long. No use asking about those.

Not to mention, the mother of one of Aiden's new sisters-in-law owned the gas station. The facts would be easy to check. He pulled his phone out of his pocket and fired off a text to Noah, asking him to track down the information with his new bride, Mikayla.

Noah responded almost immediately, saying that he was about to meet her and would ask.

Aiden refocused on Jefferson, studying his mannerisms. He kept glancing at the two-way mirror like he expected to see someone on the other side. Or was it feared he would see someone on the other side? The guy was shifty, but did that mean he was a killer?

This would be a good time to have access to Jefferson's financial records. Too bad Griff couldn't share that information if he had it.

Unless Jefferson was certain that he would be able to take over Chloe and her brother's family home and property, it wouldn't do any good to kill Nicholas or Chloe. Which didn't mean Jefferson wasn't trying.

"Did Nicholas ever lend you any money?"

Jefferson made a dramatic display out of being disgusted at the question. "No. Why would he? I never would've asked."

"How are you set up for funds?" Griff drummed his fingers on the notepad in front of him. The beat started off slow.

"I do all right." Jefferson stared at the tablet. "The information I gave you just now. Are you going to write that down?"

Griff made a show of opening his hands, palms out. "Sorry, no pen."

Jefferson scanned the room. He stared into the two-way mirror and, once again, Chloe's muscles tensed underneath Aiden's fingers. "Am I free to go?"

"You came here voluntarily, Jefferson. You can get up and walk out that door anytime you want. You don't need my permission."

The wary look that Jefferson shot Griff said he didn't believe him.

To test the waters, he stood up and crossed the room. He tried the door handle. "It's locked."

Zeus made a couple more laps around the small room.

"Is it? That's strange. Hmmm. Let me come over and try it." Griff took his time standing, and then joining Jefferson at the door. He tried the knob. "Well, look at that. Right you are. I better call one of my deputies and let him know what's going. Someone must've locked that by mistake. Mistakes happen all the time. Accidents." Griff fired off a text and then locked eyes with Jefferson. "What can you tell me about the accident on the highway last night involving Chloe Brighton?"

Jefferson backed up a couple of steps. "Nothing more than you could tell me."

"Remind me how you found out about the search party being formed?"

"It was put out on the radio and I wanted to come see for myself that my cousin was okay. I've already lost one family member and I didn't want to lose another one if there was anything I could do about it."

Griff wheeled around on Jefferson. "Did you just say someone put out on the radio that Chloe Brighton was missing?"

"Yes, sir." Jefferson studied the door. "If that deputy doesn't get here in the next five seconds, I'm going to need to speak to a lawyer."

"Where is he?" Griff locked eyes with Jefferson.

"I don't know who you're talking about."

"Really? Because I think you know exactly where Nicholas Brighton is. Let me tell you a little secret, Jefferson. We'll find him. And when we do, if there is so much as one hair on that young man's head out of place, the person who did it will regret it for the rest of his life. *Will pay* for it for the rest of his life. Now, are you trying to tell me Levi Amon is responsible for Nicholas's disappearance?"

"I'm going need to speak to that lawyer now, Sheriff."

Griff reached in his pocket and pulled out a set of keys. "Well, look here. I didn't know these were in my pocket this whole time.

What a lucky break." He unlocked the door, opened it, and then stepped aside. "Do me a favor, Jefferson. Don't leave town right now."

Jefferson pursed his lips like he was about to pop off with a comment and then seemed to think better of it. Instead, he turned away from Griff and walked out the door. Aiden closed the door to the watch room and locked it. Zeus seemed ready to break it down as Chloe tried to comfort him.

THE DOOR HANDLE to the watch room jiggled. Chloe used her hand to cover her gasp. Thankfully, Aiden had thought to lock the door.

"Can I help you with something?" Griff asked. "On second thought, Deputy Poncho, do you mind seeing Jefferson out the front door?"

"Yes, sir."

There were footsteps, the sound getting lighter and lighter as Jefferson and the deputy made their way down the hall.

"The coast is clear." Griff unlocked and opened the door.

"He seems guilty of something." Aiden took Chloe by the hand and then linked their fingers together.

Griff nodded toward his office, where the two of them, and Zeus, followed him. "You're welcome to sit down."

Chloe was too nervous, jumpy to sit still. Instead, she paced along the back wall.

"I think he's involved. I just don't know how or if he's the one who set everything up. I don't think he acted alone." Griff's cell phone rang as Chloe tried to connect the dots. Had her brother gotten involved with Kees Otilio because of Jefferson? It wasn't like her brother to just meet some random person online. Although he was trying to get his life together and with his injuries he might have felt safer talking to someone online rather than meeting them face-to-face until he got to know them.

Griff said a few *uh-huhs* and *I sees* into his phone before he ended the call. "That was Deputy Sayer. He just interviewed Kees

Otilio. The man has a rock solid alibi for last night and all day last Sunday. Turns out, he's only nineteen-years-old and has never met Nicholas face-to-face. He admitted to having some fun online, pretending to be a woman. He started talking to Nicholas about a month ago, according to his statement. Nicholas had no idea that Kees was a man. Nicholas isn't the only person that Kees has been in contact with, but he's not in a relationship with any of them. He works at the mall at a clothing store where he worked on Sunday. They received a shipment and he had to do inventory late into Sunday night. Last night, he was at his job setting up sale signs. Several of his co-workers corroborated his story, as well as his boss."

"Jefferson seemed pretty intent on bringing up Levi Amon's name." Aiden's statement came after a long, thoughtful pause. Chloe was still trying to wrap her mind around this latest news. It made sense, though. Why would someone Nicholas had met online come after her? She mentally scratched his name off the suspect list.

"I noticed that, too." That kind of information wouldn't have gotten past Griff. "I tried to make Jefferson feel as uncomfortable as I could so that I could measure his response. In my opinion, he failed miserably. Here's my dilemma. I don't have a body. I have a witness with a head injury, who claims someone with a Cajun accent attempted to...kidnap?...murder?...her." He shot an apologetic look toward Chloe as she understood what he was saying perfectly. She was an unreliable witness. Even if she did remember who attempted to hurt her and why, it wouldn't matter to a grand jury. Griff would never be able to get an indictment.

"Levi Amon is a dangerous man. What if my cousin got in over his head with him? He might've dragged Nicholas in the middle of it and Nicholas might not have been the wiser. Now Nicholas is missing and Jefferson is implicating Amon." Chloe took another couple of laps, with Zeus by her side.

"Jefferson could be trying to shine the spotlight on someone other than himself. Send us off on a tangent looking for Levi Amon. Jefferson has to know the man is difficult, if not impossible to find.

On top of that, he didn't exactly roll Amon under the bus. All he did was put the man in the vicinity on the day Nicholas disappeared."

Hope that her brother would be found alive was dwindling by the minute.

"Jefferson mentioned that he heard his cousin's name go out over the radio as a missing person." Aiden folded his arms. "I was with you when you put out that call. I don't remember you mentioning anything about Chloe by name."

"Very observant, Aiden. You're absolutely right. I didn't mention her name." So, Chloe read that as Jefferson being a boldfaced liar. She had a sinking feeling he was involved.

"We should go." If she and Aiden left now they could follow Jefferson. He might just lead them to her brother. Even though it was probably obvious to everyone, Chloe couldn't accept the fact that her brother might be gone.

"Trying to follow Jefferson won't do any good. Besides, I already have a deputy tailing him. Even Jefferson isn't stupid enough to lead us to a place where he would've stashed Nicholas. However, I put him in a panic mode on purpose. I want him to sweat."

15

"Have you thought about asking him if you can search his house?"

Chloe was pretty sure that Griff had, but she asked anyway. She couldn't help herself. Her heart was breaking for her brother and time was their enemy. All she really needed was access to Jefferson's property and Zeus. If he'd found her in the woods, she knew he could find Nicholas.

"I didn't ask because I didn't want him to realize how high on my suspect list he was. Plus, he lawyered up. There was no way he would willingly let us come onto his property after that. I played my cards the best I could. If he tries to meet with Levi Amon, we might just get a chance to nab them both at one time." What Griff wasn't saying to her was that he believed Nicholas to be dead. The implication sat thick in the air.

Walking over to Aiden, she took his hand in hers and linked their fingers. Zeus was by her side the whole way and gave her an idea. "I need fresh air. Will you take me for a ride?"

Aiden shot an apologetic look to his cousin, who seemed to know what they planned to do. Griff didn't try to stop them and she was grateful. There wasn't much he could say to her to stop her from trying to find her brother.

The minute she buckled into the seatbelt in Aiden's truck and he took the driver's side, she said, "Griff is restricted in what he can do to find my brother. He has to obey the law. I can go on my cousin's property with my dog and say that I was just stopping by to check on him. Technically, he doesn't know we were in the watch room and he won't realize that I heard everything he just said."

"It's dangerous, Chloe."

"That's why I am bringing you. I have a right to go to my cousin's house. If Nicholas is there or has been there, Zeus will know. He'll pick up on a scent." Aiden didn't say that the trail was cold or that Zeus wouldn't be able to pick up on a scent after four days, and she appreciated him for it.

"This is a longshot, Chloe. I want to make sure we make all the right moves because if Jefferson hurt Nicholas in any way, I want to make sure he spends the rest of his life in jail."

"We aren't the law. There's a chance, however small it might be, that my brother is alive and he needs my help. I can't turn my back on that, Aiden. And neither could you if this was one of your brothers. It's one of the many qualities I love about you." She reached over and let her fingers graze his shoulder. "Will you help me, please?"

Aiden started up the engine and then navigated out of the parking lot without saying a word. Neither spoke on the ride out to Jefferson's place. They couldn't have been too far behind him, ten to fifteen minutes at most and Chloe had banked on the fact that he would go home. But his car wasn't parked beside his house. So where was he?

The minute Aiden pulled alongside the house, Chloe had a feeling something was up. She hadn't been over to this side of town since returning to Gunner. Her aunt's house was on the outskirts of town.

Chloe opened the door, took in a breath and then locked eyes with Aiden. "Is that smoke?"

There was a small patch of woods behind the house. Someone

was probably burning trash illegally, but she had to make sure. She couldn't get out of the vehicle fast enough. Running through the woods with Zeus at her side brought back a memory. She remembered doing the same thing while on the run from an unknown enemy. The smell of smoke thickened, causing her to cough. And she could see black smoke billowing from what had to have been an old barn on the back of the property.

"Stay here with Zeus." Aiden barreled past her. He'd taken off his shirt and was covering his nose and mouth with it. "Stay back, Chloe. I mean it."

The smoke got to her and she started a coughing fit. She backtracked a few steps, trying to get Zeus to clean air. From what she knew about fires, which was precious little, it didn't take long for a building to go up in flames. Total destruction.

Chloe backpedaled a little more. Her right foot got caught on the scrub brush. She rolled her ankle and went tumbling backward. Zeus spun around and immediately growled. At that moment, she landed hard against something. Or someone.

The next thing she knew, she was being hauled up to standing. Strong, thick arms wrapped around her like a vise grip.

Angry words whispered in her ear chilled her blood to freezing.

"You just won't die." The sound of that voice was another slap. She instantly recognized it. *Cover up.* But it wasn't her cousin's voice. The voice belonged to Kingston Herbert.

Suddenly, his thick Cajun accent was back. Chloe tried to jerk free from his grasp. He laughed in response.

"I don't think so, sweetheart." And then she felt it. Cold. Metal. A knife against her throat. "You just couldn't leave it alone, could you?"

"Where's my brother?" Thoughts of self-defense maneuvers ran through Chloe's head, none of them useful in this situation. If she tried to break free now, he could accidentally slit her throat. But then, he planned to do that anyway.

Zeus unleashed a torrent of barks and growls that strung together. The houses here sat on acre lots. She doubted anyone could hear or would care. Folks on this side of town always had a mind-their-own-business approach.

She glanced toward the structure and tried to wriggle free from Kingston's hands.

"I want you to watch your brother and your boyfriend die together."

"Why not kill Nicholas already? Why keep him around this long?"

"If it had been up to me, he would already be dead. Your cousin thought he might be useful if you didn't play long." They'd intended to use Nicholas to draw her out all along? If a body had turned up, she would've stopped looking. This way, they kept her out and about and could make an easy case for an 'accident' meant to take her life.

"Aiden won't die in there and neither will my brother."

"The door is locked, Chloe. They don't have a choice."

No matter what else happened, Kingston was going to end her life. There was no way in hell she planned to make it easy on him.

Zeus chose that moment to lunge toward Kingston. She managed to swivel her hips enough to get out the way. She could almost hear the bite as Zeus clamped onto Kingston's thigh. Taking advantage of the distraction, she pushed Kingston's arm away and ducked out of his grasp. The knife barely sliced her. It felt more like a paper cut that anything else. She didn't care. Couldn't care. Because the knife in Kingston's hand was about to come down on Zeus.

"No." She grabbed his forearm with both hands and sank her own teeth into his flesh.

He shouted a few choice words but the knife came tumbling out of his hand. She heard Zeus yelp and prayed that he was okay. There was no time to assess injuries. Zeus's bites came in rapid succession and she heard Kingston shout out in pain.

Torn between leaving Zeus to fight Kingston alone and the possibility of saving Aiden and her brother, Chloe search for the biggest rock she could find. She found one that fit in her palm, tossed it, and nailed Kingston in the head. Blood squirted from his forehead, but he caught hold of her hand in the process. It was almost too easy for him to send her flying. Her head missed a tree by less than a foot.

She scrambled up on all fours and felt around for anything else she could use. Another yelp from Zeus got her feet moving. She grabbed the only thing she could find, which was a sharp stick.

Repeatedly, she jabbed Kingston with it as Zeus managed to wrestle the big man onto his back. And then Zeus went flying off of him with a yelp. He was back on his feet and lunging toward Kingston within a few seconds.

Kingston was feeling around for the knife and she could see that he almost had it. So, she ran over and jabbed his hand with a sharp stick as hard as she could. As she tried to grab the knife's handle, he knocked Zeus off a third time and then sat upright. She was within reach. Easy reach. Chloe readied herself to take another hit.

And then from behind her, she heard coughing. She was pretty certain she heard Aiden's voice and her heart leapt. Kingston must've seen him coming because he made a last-ditch effort to get the knife. But he was no match for Aiden.

The next few seconds happened so fast and yet so oddly slow, like a movie playing out in slow motion. Aiden was on top of Kingston, his thighs pinning him to the ground. Aiden managed to get his cell phone out of his pocket and was calling for emergency services. Zeus was slow to get up and she could see that he was panting heavily.

She thought he was coming toward her until he passed her. She spun around and saw a sight that she'd been certain she would never see again not an hour ago. Nicholas. Her brother. Alive.

Aiden had set him down next to a tree. Nicholas's head hung forward, limp. She ran to her brother and checked that he was breathing. Satisfied that he was, tears sprang to her eyes as she watched Zeus lick Nicholas's face and her brother responded by lifting his hand toward his dog.

Nicholas was alive. Alive. She repeated the phrase a few times in her head, so she would believe it.

Before she could process everything happening, she heard sirens. And then she heard voices and what sounded like an army of responders coming at them from all directions. Somehow, Griff was there and it was his knee being jammed into Kingston's back after Aiden flipped him over. Kingston's hands were jacked up behind his back, his wrists zip cuffed.

Only when he was secured and no longer a threat did Aiden find his way to her. A pair of EMTs were working on Nicholas, strapping him onto a small gurney. Firefighters ran past as she sat there on her bottom, holding her brother's hand, fighting the wave of nausea from all the activity. Her adrenaline spike was wearing off and her body was starting to shake.

The sight of Aiden, alive, when she thought for certain she'd lost him caused emotional floodgates to open. He took a knee beside her. His hands cupped her cheeks and he looked at her with so much love in his eyes.

"I thought I lost you."

She could've said the same thing if she had the energy to speak.

"I love you, Chloe. I can't lose you again. I won't survive it this time."

Before she could respond, her brother was being lifted and the EMTs started to sprint back toward the house. She moved her hand off Zeus's fur and saw blood.

After about a half-second, Aiden scooped Zeus up in his arms. "Are you okay to walk?"

She nodded. Even if she wasn't, she didn't care. Nothing would stop her from making sure Zeus survived. Her brother was already in the hands of the most capable people. Zeus deserved the same treatment.

By the time they made it back to the house, the place was surrounded by emergency vehicles. She watched as Kingston was tossed into the back seat of Griff's service vehicle. Griff slammed the door closed.

"Where can I set him down?" Aiden shouted the question. An EMT ran over with a blanket and placed it on the ground.

"I'm no vet, but I'm trained in emergency medicine and I'm happy to take a look at your friend there," the EMT said.

Aiden nodded after gently placing Zeus on the folded blanket.

The EMT went to work checking Zeus thoroughly. He cleaned a

couple of spots of blood and put a little bit of ointment on three cuts. Satisfied with his work, he sat back on his heels. "That's a great dog you have there. None of his injuries are serious. He should heal up just fine. I put a little antibiotic on him that should last until you get him to his vet."

"I can't thank you enough." Aiden shook the EMTs hand.

"You're welcome." With that, the EMT stood up and then jogged over to his team.

Nicholas was loaded up and the doors were closed before Chloe had time to process. As the driver rounded the back, heading toward the driver seat, he looked to Chloe and Aiden. "We promise to take good care of him. We'll see you at the hospital."

Relief with hearing those words was a tsunami. Chloe blew out a breath and sank down a little bit.

Griff jogged over. "Do you two need a ride to the hospital? One of my deputies can take you while I make sure this jerk is locked up next to your cousin."

"You found Jefferson?" Chloe didn't bother to mask her shock.

"He was on the highway headed toward Mexico. After I put a BOLO out, he wasn't hard to find. He confessed to panicking after he left my office and telling Kingston to set the barn on fire. Turns out, Kingston started using narcotics again and your cousin found out about it. He was bribing Kingston with the promise of a portion of his inheritance. He said he was ready to take what he believed belonged to him. He said his mother sold the place to your parents a long time ago and always regretted it because it became more valuable than the land she kept for herself."

Chloe couldn't fathom the kind of jerk who would kill over money.

"Jefferson was having trouble paying his bills. He saw Nicholas's situation as a way to dig himself out." Griff offered Aiden a hand up. He took it. The two embraced. "We all have our own stuff to deal with, cousin. But I hope we'll be spending a lot more time together from now on."

"You can count on it." Aiden turned to Chloe and brought the backs of his fingers up to her cheek. He gently stroked her face. "I can get down on one knee if you want me to. In fact, you could pretty much tell me anything you wanted me to do right now and I'd do it. You're my best friend, Chloe Brighton.. But more than that, I realized a long time ago that I'm in love with you. I want to spend the rest of my life with you. It would do me a great honor if you would agree to become my bride. I want to spend the rest of my life showing you how much you mean to me. If you say yes, Chloe, I promise never to let go."

The tears welling in Chloe's eyes were tears of joy. She pressed a tender kiss to Aiden's lips. "I can't imagine spending my life any other way than with my best friend and the man I've been in love with since the day we met. So, yes. I'll marry you, Aiden Quinn. And I'll spend the rest of my life loving you."

Aiden pulled her into an embrace. Right then. Right there. The rest of their life together began.

16

EPILOGUE

Eli Quinn had tucked the invitation to his brother's wedding into his nightstand before heading downtown and to the playground with his kids. He had no qualms about attending Aiden and Chloe's wedding next month. In fact, six of his brothers had found the happiness with a partner that Eli couldn't seem to give his ex-wife, Camille.

The Fort Worth socialite had convinced him that she'd had fallen in love with the ranch, with him. He'd gone all-in. Hook, line, and sinker. They'd had two children together after a whirlwind courtship before she decided she didn't love him anymore and couldn't handle ranch life. Their entire relationship had played out in three short years.

He'd been a sucker because he loved his wife. He'd done his level best to make her happy and his ego was still bruised from the failure. At least he got the two most amazing kids in the world out of the deal. Camille had walked away from Oliver and Olivia without so much as a backward glance, giving him full custody and requesting zero visitation.

Trying to figure out how he'd let himself fall for someone who didn't return the sentiment or could be so indifferent toward her own kids had been an exercise in futility. Eli had miscalculated. It wasn't the kind of mistake he normally made.

Licking his wounds would do no good. Eli had decided a long time ago that life was a lot like using a car's navigation system. There were times when directions were confusing, and he took a wrong turn. On the road, he was able to correct his mistake and get back on course, smarter.

Committing to a path had been the missing piece in Camille. She wasn't the settling down type. Last he'd heard, she moved on to an oil tycoon in Houston where she currently lived. Eli figured the relationship would play out in a similar fashion. Camille wasn't the kind of person who could settle in for the long haul. Eli's only regret was that he'd cost his children a mother by not realizing it sooner. The situation was a catch-22.

Without question, Eli would trade his life for his kiddos. Blessed didn't begin to describe how he felt with those two angels in his life. Not being able to give them a mother at all, let alone one they deserved, would always be a knife to the chest—and history repeating itself?

As Eli pushed his little girl on the swing at the downtown Gunner playground, he could only hope he would be enough for her and her brother. The thought of bringing another person into their world who could turn tail and walk out again wasn't even a consideration. Between rising at four a.m. for ranch work and taking care of Oliver and Olivia, he didn't have much energy left for dating anyway.

So, he was caught off guard when a stray lightning bolt struck his chest the minute he caught sight of a stranger holding an infant in her arms while sitting on a nearby swing. He didn't want to notice her heart-shaped face or how shiny her blacker-than-the-night-sky hair was as sunbeams reflected off it. Her fashionable ripped jeans didn't exactly scream stability. Even though he didn't get off the ranch much, it was easy to see she was new in town and most likely passing through.

Chin to chest, he also realized she was trying to hide the fact she was crying. He would probably regret this action, but he couldn't help himself. Eli picked up his smiling, babbling daughter and walked over to introduce himself.

To FIND out what happens to Eli and Emory, click here.

ALSO BY BARB HAN

Don't Mess With Texas Cowboys

Texas Cowboy Justice

Texas Cowboy's Honor

Texas Cowboy Daddy

Texas Cowboy's Baby

Texas Cowboy's Bride

Texas Cowboy's Family

Cowboys of Cattle Cove

Cowboy Reckoning

Cowboy Cover-up

Cowboy Retribution

Cowboy Judgment

Cowboy Conspiracy

Cowboy Rescue

Cowboy Target

Crisis: Cattle Barge

Sudden Setup

Endangered Heiress

Texas Grit

Kidnapped at Christmas

Murder and Mistletoe

Bulletproof Christmas

For more of Barb's books, visit www.BarbHan.com.

ABOUT THE AUTHOR

Barb Han is a USA TODAY and Publisher's Weekly Bestselling Author. Reviewers have called her books "heartfelt" and "exciting."

Barb lives in Texas--her true north--with her adventurous family, a poodle mix and a spunky rescue who is often referred to as a hot mess. She is the proud owner of too many books (if there is such a thing). When not writing, she can be found exploring Manhattan, on a mountain either hiking or skiing depending on the season, or swimming in her own backyard.

Made in the USA
Monee, IL
13 February 2023

27592024R00090